GIRLS
TO THE
RESCUE®
BOOK #7

*Tales of clever, courageous girls
from around the world*

EDITED BY BRUCE LANSKY

 **Meadowbrook Press**

Distributed by Simon & Schuster
New York

Library of Congress Catalog Card Number: 95-17733

Publisher's ISBN: 0-88166-377-8
Simon & Schuster Ordering # 0-689-84079-9

Editor: Bruce Lansky
Coordinating Editors: Jason Sanford, Megan McGinnis
Copyeditor: Christine Zuchora-Walske
Proofreader: Angela Wiechmann
Production Manager: Paul Woods
Production Assistant: Danielle White
Cover Illustrator: Joy Allen

p. 1 "On the Way to Broken Bow © 2000 by Marianne J. Dyson; p. 15 "Reni and the
Tiger" © 2000 by Timothy Tocher; p. 25 "Abbie's Light" © 2000 by Tenna Leigh; p.
35 "Troop 13 to the Rescue" © 2000 by Penny Warner; p. 53 "The Treasure beneath
the Hay" © 2000 by Nancy Alpert Mower; p. 69 "Firedance" © 2000 by Bonnie
Brightman; p. 82 "Taneya's Best Shot" © 2000 by Debra Tracy; p. 96 "Ayasha's
Arrow" © 2000 by Mary Houlgate.

Published by Meadowbrook Press, 5451 Smetana Drive, Minnetonka, MN 55343
www.meadowbrookpress.com

BOOK TRADE DISTRIBUTION by Simon & Schuster, a division of Simon and
Schuster, Inc., 1230 Avenue of the Americas, New York, NY 10020

03 02 01 00   12 11 10 9 8 7 6 5 4 3 2 1

Printed in the United States of America

Dedication

This book is dedicated to my daughter, Dana. I used to make up stories when she was young, hoping to inspire her to believe in herself and to pursue her dreams. It is in that spirit that I have written and collected the stories in this series.

Acknowledgments

Thank you to the following young women who served
on a reading panel for this project:

Heather Adams, Makensie Allex, Heidi Allstop, Hayley Anderson,
Rachel Armstrong, Erica Bezotte, Katelyn Boser, Jackie Brown,
Brittney Bruzek, Samantha Byrne-Bitzan, Sarah Byrne-Bitzan,
Andrea Carlson, Christie Carlson, Katie Casey, Brianna Christensen,
Ruthie Christianson, Catherine Colwell, Demi Cooper, Joanna
Desautels, Natalie Dimberg, Jenny Dvorak, Breanna Ellsworth, Sahar
Elmtalab, Sara Engler, Liz Ennis, Brianna Erstad, Jenny Ford, Megan
Frank, Marisa Fredrickson, Jessica Gethardt, Heather Gilbertson,
Mary Gleisberg, Paula Gleisberg, Emily Goplen, Beth Gucinski,
Samantha Halpern, Elizabeth Hawkinson, Jessica Hendrix, Holly
Hlavacek, Amandla Hunter, Jennifer Hurd, Amanda Impola, Melissa
Johnson, Kasey Jones, Marie Jubert, Kelsey Kelly, Jessica Kempe,
Allyson Kihle, Kristin Kordovsky, Christie Kostreba, Meghan Kunz,
Becca Krauss, Nicole LaPoint, Sarah Larson, Randi Launderville,
Stacey Lillebo, Jennie Lillemo, Hannah Lindquist, Susie Lorence,
Amanda Lyons, Megan Magdzas, Paige Maki, Kayla McNab, Jena
Megel, Morgan Mitchell, Ellen Moleski, Nicole Moleski, Elizabeth
Muenchow, Emily Mumma, Katelyn Murray, Ali Myhre, Anna
Myhre, Rebecca Ney, Kaylee Olson, Elizabeth Poole, Sarah Rolson,
Katie Samson, Zoe Setright, Lina Sieverling, Maura Sokol, Amanda
Solyntjes, Krista Sorensen, Gina Stewart, Kascie Sturtevant, Emma
Swanson, Leah Thielmann, Alissa Tousignant, Tarra Traut, Rachael
Turner, JoAnn Tyrdik, Sarah VanSanten, Laurie Verant, Vanessa
Wagner, Abby Warmboe, Caitlin Webb, Alissa Wilkerson, Kristen
Wood, Rachel Worthington, Tiffany Zacher

Contents

Introduction

When you look at this book's cover illustration, you can guess that the pilot has passed out and that the plane is being flown by a girl. What you can't tell is that Kimberly, the girl flying the plane through a thunderstorm, has lost the use of her legs. "On the Way to Broken Bow" is the first of many exciting stories in *Girls to the Rescue Book #7*. All are about girls who save the day—whether it's saving gorillas from a poacher's snare or saving a brother from a wildfire.

In the second story, "Reni and the Tiger," a tiger threatens a Sumatran village. Unfortunately, the villagers cannot shoot the tiger—it's protected by environmental laws. So it's up to Reni to find a way to rid the village of the dangerous "striped one" without breaking any laws.

In "Abbie's Light" the daughter of a lighthouse keeper must keep the beacon lit during a violent storm while her father is away and her injured mother recuperates. As the storm worsens, Abbie uses what's at hand to save her family before the sea swallows their home.

The exciting story "Troop 13 to the Rescue" takes place at a scout camp where a rappelling competition is being held. When the rope of the fastest girl catches on a sharp rock and begins to fray, second-place Jonnie, with victory now in sight, decides that winning the race isn't the most important thing.

"The Treasure beneath the Hay" tells the story of Goldie, a Jewish girl from Odessa, who helps her family smuggle her brothers out of Russia. If soldiers find the boys, they will draft them into the army and send them to the front lines, from which they may never return. Goldie rises to the occasion when soldiers approach her family's wagon three times.

When a wildfire sweeps down a mesa toward her home, Angelita, a young Mexican-American girl, quickly and cleverly figures out how she and her younger brother can escape the flames and save their home in "Firedance."

Taneya's father is ranger at Volcanoes National Park in Rwanda. She loves watching the gorillas with her father and particularly loves Raisin, a baby gorilla she has named. When poachers set snares that endanger Raisin and her kin, Taneya finds a highly creative way to save them in "Taneya's Best Shot."

"Ayasha's Arrow" tells the story of a young Anishinabe girl who would rather hunt with the men than learn the "womanly arts" of sewing and weaving like her big sister. She practices archery in secret until one day when she must use her skill to save two lives—even though she risks the disapproval of her father and the rest of the clan.

I hope you find all the stories in this book both entertaining and inspiring. I also hope you take away the message that you, too, can rise to the occasion and help your friends, family, and community when they are in need.

Bruce Lansky

On the Way to Broken Bow

AN ORIGINAL STORY BY MARIANNE J. DYSON

Airplane Jargon:
Roger: word used in radio communications that means "message received."

It wasn't the best day for flying in a small plane. The air was bouncy, and scattered storm clouds made an obstacle course of the route between Fort Worth, Texas, and Broken Bow, Oklahoma. Kimberly didn't mind. She loved to fly with her mom; in an airplane, her wheelchair didn't hold her back. But their eleven-year-old passenger, Cohita, was scared. The girl's eyes looked enormous amid all the white bandages protecting her burned skin.

Kimberly's mom flew with Angel Flight, a group of volunteer pilots who carried patients to and from hospitals around the country free of charge. Cohita had just been released from a burn center in Texas, and Kimberly's mom was flying her home to Broken Bow. Kimberly's job was to help Cohita feel at ease during her first flight in a small plane.

But the weather was making Kimberly's job difficult today. At every flash of distant lightning, Cohita yelped, reminded of the flash fire that had burned her face and scalp. Kimberly needed to get her thinking about something else.

"Hey, Cohita," Kimberly called. Cohita looked up from the stuffed bear the social workers had given her. Kimberly held up an aviation map. "See these blue tepees?" Cohita nodded. "These are symbols for towers. The tallest one is 987 feet. If we can find it, we'll know exactly where we are. Want to help?"

"I guess so," Cohita said.

Kimberly smiled. "Great! It should have blinking red lights on top."

Almost immediately Cohita asked, "Is that it over

there?"

Kimberly looked where Cohita pointed. She couldn't spot the tower, so she lifted a pair of binoculars to her eyes. There it was blinking steadily in the distance. "Wow, you must have the eyes of an eagle!" she said.

"Yes, but it doesn't matter," Cohita mumbled.

Kimberly frowned. "Why do you say that?"

"Because I'm a monster!" Cohita wailed. "I will never have any friends." She sighed and hung her head.

Kimberly's mother glanced over. Kimberly nodded and said, "I thought that, too, right after my accident."

Cohita's head jerked up. Kimberly plunged into her story. "It happened at summer camp. I was nine. Some girls I thought were my friends dared me to pet Black Lightning, a wild stallion. They were mad at me, I guess, and wanted to get me in trouble for being in the stallion's pen." Even after four years, the memory stung. "He reared up and landed right on top of me. I'll never forget the sound of that moment: laughter, Black Lightning's terrified neighing, and the *snap* of my spine."

"That's horrible!" Cohita said.

Kimberly nodded. "Some friends, huh? And the

girls who told you to wash your hair with gasoline . . . It's better to have no friends than friends like that."

Cohita stared down at her bear. "I was stupid to listen to them. They said it would make my hair thick and shiny." Cohita blotted her eyes with a tissue. "Now I have no hair at all!"

Kimberly knew that helpless feeling all too well. "There's nothing you can do about that," she said gently. "You have to focus on things you *can* do." The plane jostled a bit in the turbulent air. "Like using those eagle eyes to help me find where we are on the map."

Kimberly's mom smiled. "Speaking of maps, will you hold the yoke for me while I search under the seat for the next one?"

"Sure!" Kimberly said.

"What's a yoke?" Cohita asked.

"A yoke is a steering wheel," Kimberly said. "There are two and they work together. That way either the pilot or the copilot can fly the plane." Kimberly turned her yoke to the right, and her mother's yoke turned right, too. "See?"

"Like two friends, always dancing together—" Cohita stopped herself and looked apologetically at Kimberly, who would never dance. "I'm sorry!" Cohita said. "I didn't mean . . ."

"It's okay," Kimberly said. "I'd rather fly than dance anyway!"

While they were talking, Kimberly's mother undid her shoulder harness and dug a map out from under her seat. "Broken Bow, Oklahoma, is right here," she said, handing the map to Cohita. "We should get there in thirty minutes."

"Thank you again, Mrs. Gonzales," Cohita said, taking the map. "My parents couldn't afford an air ambulance, and the doctors said I might pick up germs on a long bus trip. If it weren't for Angel Flight, I don't know how I'd get home."

"I was glad to volunteer," Kimberly's mom said. She was reaching for her shoulder harness when a warning light caught her eye. "Oh darn!" she said. "The alternator is out."

"What does that mean?" Kimberly asked.

"It means the engine isn't charging the battery anymore. When the battery runs out, the lights and radios will quit. But don't worry; we're almost there, and I don't need the lights and radios to land anyway." She was reaching for her shoulder harness again when—*wham!*—the plane dropped like a broken elevator. The yoke jerked from Kimberly's hands, then she blacked out.

Kimberly awoke to Cohita screaming. The plane was bouncing like a bucking bronco. "Wh-at hap-pen-ed?" Kimberly stuttered in the shaking plane. Then she saw her mother slumped sideways with a nasty gash on the top of her head.

"Mom! Wake up!" Kimberly shouted, tugging on her mother's arm. With her shoulder harness off, she must have slammed into the ceiling! Kimberly's stomach rose in her throat.

"Do something!" Cohita shouted.

Kimberly grabbed the yoke and pulled back with all her strength. "We must have hit a wind shear," she said. A wind shear was like a waterfall in the air, caused when one air mass ran into another. At least the plane had not slammed all the way to the ground. Kimberly pressed the talk button on the yoke and spoke into her headset's microphone. "Whoever's on the radio, this is Cessna 1-2-1-niner foxtrot. We have an emergency!"

"1-2-1-niner foxtrot, this is Forth Worth Radio. Please state nature of emergency and give altitude."

Kimberly looked at the altimeter. "We're at 2,300

feet." They had dropped over 2,000 feet already! "I think we hit a wind shear. My mom, the pilot, has been knocked out." Kimberly was not quite successful in keeping the squeak out of her voice.

"1-niner fox, we have you on radar. You are about 15 miles southwest of Idabel airport. Don't worry; we'll talk you in."

"Okay," Kimberly said. When she pressed the talk button, the glowing numbers on the radio blinked. The alternator! "Fort Worth, Mom said the alternator was out, and just now the radio lights blinked when I pushed the talk button. Can you hear me?"

"1-niner fox, roger, we can hear you. Stay calm; we'll have instructions for you in a minute."

Kimberly grabbed the yoke to stop a roll to the right. But she overcontrolled, and they banked left. Fists of water punched the plane, which had wandered into a thunderstorm. Lightning struck nearby. Cohita screamed.

"Stop that!" Kimberly yelled. "I'm scared enough without you screaming!"

Cohita went silent. The sounds of the droning engine and pelting rain filled the cockpit. "Mom, please wake up!" Kimberly cried.

With one hand on the yoke, Kimberly fished out the first-aid kit and pressed some gauze to her mom's head to stop the bleeding. She used her mom's headset to hold the gauze in place.

"1-niner fox, my name is Mitch. Who am I talking to?"

This was a new voice. Kimberly thought he sounded kind of like Grandpa. "This is Kimberly Gonzales," she said.

"Hi, Kimberly. Mind if I ask how old you are?"

"Thirteen."

"Great age, thirteen," he said. "I started flying when I was thirteen. 'Course, that was a long time ago."

"He's trying to calm me down," Kimberly thought. She realized just how nervous she was. Had she really yelled at Cohita?

"First, because of your alternator problem, I want you to keep your radio use to a minimum. The battery might last long enough to get you down, but every time you transmit, it drains it. Say 'yes' if you understand."

"Yes," Kimberly said. How would she get through this if she lost the radio?

"Good," Mitch said. "The next thing we need to do is bring you down to 2,000 feet. All you have to do is pull back a little on the throttle. If you understand, say 'yes' again."

Kimberly's voice bounced with the plane. "Y-ee-ss," she said. She yanked the throttle, and the engine grew quieter. Her stomach jumped into her throat.

"You're descending a bit faster than you need to," Mitch said.

A bit! Kimberly knew those flight controllers were masters of understatement. She must be falling like a brick. Kimberly pulled back on the yoke to raise the airplane's nose, then pushed the throttle in a little bit to give the engine more gas. Her stomach settled at about heart level.

"Great flying, Ace," Mitch said.

Kimberly had a feeling he'd have said that no matter what she did. But she had to admit, this guy knew how to make her feel better.

"Okay, pilot Kimberly, if the fuel mixture knob is not already pushed in all the way, push it in. It's the red knob right next to the throttle."

"I see it." Kimberly pushed the knob in. A gust of wind tossed the plane, and her mom fell forward against the yoke. The plane went into a nosedive!

"Kimberly, I recommend you pull back on the yoke to stop your descent," Mitch said.

"I'm trying!" The yoke wouldn't budge with her mom's weight against it. Just as Kimberly was about to remove her shoulder harness, Cohita reached forward and grabbed Mrs. Gonzales's left arm, pulling her off the yoke. Then she fastened Mrs. Gonzales's shoulder harness. "Cohita, you're out of your seat belt!" Kimberly shouted. "You could be knocked out!"

"So could you," Cohita yelled back. "Then who would fly the plane?"

Kimberly hadn't thought about that. She pulled back the yoke and swallowed nervously. "Thank you, Cohita. And," she added, "I'm sorry I yelled at you."

"It's okay. You were right. I was only thinking of how scared I was instead of how I could help."

"Thanks again," Kimberly said. She'd only lost a few hundred feet thanks to Cohita.

Mitch said, "Kimberly, do you see the airport?"

"No," Kimberly said. "But a red flag just came up on an instrument in front of me."

"It means it's not working. That's okay. You're real close to the airport. Descend to 1,500 feet. Understand?"

"Yes," Kimberly said. Her lower lip quivered in fear. If the instruments weren't working, how long would the radio last?

"You're doing great," Mitch said. "The airport is to your left. Look for a bright beacon flashing green then white. Tell me when you see it."

Kimberly didn't see anything but rain. A gust jerked the plane up then down, and lightning flashed nearby. At least Cohita didn't scream this time. But how could Kimberly land at an airport she couldn't find?

"Cohita, I need those eagle eyes of yours. The airport's to the left, but I can't see it. Try to spot a light that flashes green then white."

"Yes!" Cohita said, pointing to the front. "I can see the light through the propeller!"

Kimberly tilted the nose down and peered into the rain. She couldn't see anything, but she trusted Cohita. She turned the plane in the direction Cohita was pointing. "I see it!" Kimberly said. She flashed a smile back at Cohita.

"Good," Mitch said. "But listen: If the radio fails, just keep descending to the runway. When you get over the big number 35 at the end of the runway, your altitude should be between 50 and 100 feet. Also, watch the air speed indicator. If you're going under 60 miles per hour, push the yoke forward or the throttle in a bit to pick up some speed. Got it?"

Kimberly gulped. "I think so." There was so much to remember!

"You're a bit too high. You need to—"

"Mitch?" Kimberly thumbed the talk switch. Nothing! The radio had gone dark. Need to what? If she were too high, she'd go past the runway. There were buildings there! Her altitude was 300 feet—wasn't it supposed to be 50 to 100? She needed to lose altitude fast.

Lightning lit up the wing. The flaps! They would help her descend fast without taking a nosedive. She pulled the lever. Whoa! Talk about dropping like a brick!

The ground seemed to rise at her. The plane hit hard and sped down the runway. What was that ahead? A deer! Unless she turned the plane, she was going to hit it! But the only way to steer on the ground was to use the rudder pedals. Kimberly's feet dangled uselessly. If she could only reach the pedals with her arms . . . The tow bar!

"Cohita—quick! I need the tow bar. It's on the floor by your feet!"

"I see it!" Cohita said. She handed the metal bar to Kimberly.

Kimberly jammed the bar against the rudder pedal.

The plane skidded to the left, avoiding the deer. However, there wasn't time to change directions, and the plane sped off the runway into a grassy ditch. The landing gear smashed into some runway lights, jerking the plane to a violent stop with the left wing striking the ground. The cockpit was undamaged, and they were all alive. But fuel spurted out of the wing and burst into flames. Kimberly shut off the engine. It was eerily quiet.

Fire crackled and popped outside her mother's door. Luckily, there was a door on Kimberly's side, too. Her heart pounded. She couldn't move her mother; she couldn't even lift herself. She needed to follow her own advice and focus on what she could do.

Kimberly undid her seat belt and popped the door. Rain whipped in and soaked her.

"Cohita, I need you to climb over the seat. Cohita?" She didn't answer. Kimberly turned to see her staring wide-eyed at the flames. Kimberly reached back and yanked the bear from her grip to get her attention. "Cohita, snap out of it! You're okay. Undo your seat belt and climb out!"

Cohita blinked, then began fumbling with her seat belt. In a few minutes, she had climbed out and dragged Kimberly away from the plane. Kimberly handed the bear back to her.

"What about your mother?" Cohita asked.

"She's too heavy for us," Kimberly said. "But now that we're out of the way, rescue workers can get to her more quickly."

She was right. In just a few minutes, a fire truck showed up. Two firefighters jumped off and ran to rescue her mother. They soon pulled her clear and put out the fire.

"Thank you, Kimberly," Cohita said, her wet hand squeezing Kimberly's. An ambulance pulled up.

"For landing the plane?" Kimberly asked. She watched as they loaded her mother onto a stretcher. "You helped a lot. Besides, we didn't have much choice."

"Yes we did," Cohita said. "We could have just given up. You showed me that I can do things even if I am burned."

"You can," Kimberly agreed, pushing wet hair out of her eyes. "Including making new friends—real friends—when you get back to Broken Bow. You'll know they're real friends because when you're around them, you'll forget about your problems."

Lightning flashed. Cohita didn't scream. Instead, she smiled.

Reni and the Tiger

AN ORIGINAL STORY BY TIMOTHY TOCHER

Reni and her grandfather lived at the edge of a beautiful rain forest on the island of Sumatra. Grandfather knew the secret places where precious orchids grew. He and Reni gathered the rare and beautiful blossoms and sold them to the tourist hotels in nearby Palembang.

One late October morning, Reni and Grandfather were wending their way through the forest toward a spot where huge purple orchids grew from the trunks of trees. It would be Reni's job to climb the trees and carefully cut loose the fragile blossoms.

Reni drank in the morning sunshine. She found it hard to imagine that the monsoon season would soon bring drenching rains.

The two had been walking for perhaps an hour when Grandfather bent to examine some animal droppings on the path. He straightened abruptly, signaled Reni to be silent, and turned toward home. He didn't say a word until they were back in their little hut.

"Grandfather, what is wrong?" Reni asked. "Why did we come home with empty baskets on such a fine day?"

"The ruler of the forest is back, Reni. It is not safe to gather orchids while he remains."

"What ruler, Grandfather?"

"The striped cat, the one all animals fear, the one who fears nothing," he answered.

"A tiger? I've never seen one!" Reni said excitedly.

"Do not speak his name!" Grandfather scolded. He cracked open the door to their hut and peeked into the yard. "My father taught me that if you call the great cat, he will come."

Reni didn't believe that old superstition, but she peeked around Grandfather just the same. The garden was empty, and their goat grazed peacefully in the yard.

"How will we gather orchids if the t—," Reni began,

"if the striped cat is here to stay?"

"I must think," said Grandfather. "In my father's day, there were many such dangers."

"I'll catch some fish for our dinner." Reni headed off Grandfather's reminder, "And I won't go into the forest."

Reni walked to the bank of the River Baro where her bamboo raft was moored. She climbed aboard, then reached over and released the metal hook that anchored the raft to a tree stump.

The raft drifted on the gentle current. Reni dropped her line into the water and waited. She thought of the coming monsoon. It would turn this little stream into a raging torrent.

Within an hour, Reni had caught enough catfish to feed herself and Grandfather, plus a few for anyone in the village who might need them. She used a pole to push her raft upstream.

When she returned to the hut, she found Muladi, the huntsman, with her grandfather. Muladi hunted deer and wild pigs in the forest and sold the meat to the hotels. She offered him several fish, which he gladly accepted. Grandfather held up the fine steaks that Muladi had brought, and Reni thanked him.

"Muladi, too, is worried about our visitor,"

Grandfather said. "We can't think of a solution."

"Could you shoot the—," Reni caught herself, "the visitor?" she asked Muladi.

"The government thinks more of the big cat than it does of its people," Muladi sighed. "The law protects him from my gun but does not protect me from his teeth and claws."

"Then maybe the government will remove the visitor," Reni said.

Muladi smiled. "Maybe it will. I will ask my nephew to look into it. Maybe the government will take the striped one to the National Park, where he belongs."

Muladi's nephew lived in Palembang and earned his living buying orchids, game, and other riches of the rain forest from the villagers and reselling them to the hotels. Muladi bowed to Grandfather, smiled at Reni, and left carrying his string of fish.

For a few days, Grandfather and Reni worked in the garden, staying away from the forest and the dangerous visitor. When Muladi returned, his head hung low.

"My nephew talked to the officials in Palembang," he said. "They would love to have our visitor in the National Park, but there is no money to come and capture him. Unless we can convince him to swim twenty miles downriver, he will remain our guest indefinitely."

"We can't shoot him, and the government won't trap him. What can we do?" Reni asked.

"Perhaps when the monsoon begins and the hunting is poor, he will leave us," said Muladi.

"Or maybe when the hunting is poor, he will come to visit our village," Grandfather said. Reni shivered.

The rains began right on schedule, and whole days were lost to the downpours. Reni and Grandfather lashed the raft to the hut in case the River Baro overflowed its banks. Reni spent her time catching up on indoor chores and listening to Grandfather's stories.

There had been no sign of the visitor for days, and the villagers began to hope that he had left the area. Then the bleat of a goat woke Reni in the middle of the night.

She started to rise from her mat, but Grandfather placed a hand on her chest. He leaned close and whispered, "It is the great cat."

Although she strained her ears, Reni heard no other sound. She didn't remember falling asleep. When she opened her eyes again, the sun was shining brightly in the hut. Remembering the goat, she jumped up.

She found Grandfather in the yard. He pointed at the bloody ground. The cat had killed the goat, then dragged it across the clearing and into the forest.

"Our poor nanny," Reni sighed. "We must do something, Grandfather. The visitor has taken our orchid business and our goat. If he stays, we may starve."

"If only the monsoon would wash him down the river!" Grandfather said.

Reni didn't answer; she had an idea. "Does Muladi have any game?" she asked.

Grandfather shrugged. "Between the monsoon and the visitor, there has been little opportunity for hunting."

"I'll go see him after breakfast," Reni said.

Grandfather looked at her curiously. Then he announced, "And I will work on a project. I remember something my father taught me about the visitor."

Reni was back by noon, carrying a rotting haunch of deer from Muladi. She knew the big cat was probably asleep at this hot time of day, but she was still relieved to get home safely.

When she entered the hut, Grandfather held up a wooden mask. The face looked very much like Reni's.

"What is that for, Grandfather?" Reni asked as she

set the rancid meat near the door.

"This mask is worn on the back of the head," Grandfather said as he lowered the mask onto Reni. "My father always wore one into the forest. He believed that our visitor would never attack a person from the front, so someone with two faces would be safe."

"Why did you make this for me?" Reni asked innocently.

"Because I know you have some plan to get rid of our visitor," Grandfather answered, "and that no matter what I say, you will try to carry it out. I want to give you some protection"

"I'll wear your mask, Grandfather. But hopefully our visitor will be more interested in this smelly meat than in me."

That evening, Reni hung Grandfather's mask from her neck. Grandfather helped her carry the raft to the swollen river. Holding the stinking meat, she jumped aboard. The current grabbed the raft, and it raced downstream.

The rain fell steadily. Reni fought with her pole to stay near shore. She managed to steer the raft down the branch of the Baro that flowed through the rain forest. She rode until she recognized the area where

Grandfather had found the visitor's droppings.

Reni picked up the metal hook she used for an anchor and threw it into the thick brush along the shore. The raft stopped when the rope pulled tight. She grabbed the rope that was tied to the raft and pulled hand over hand, tugging the raft out of the current and toward the shore.

Reni struggled to keep her balance. Though she was a strong swimmer, she wasn't sure she could fight the rain-swollen current if she fell in. Finally, she was close enough to jump to the bank. She left the rotting meat on the raft.

Reni found the hook and threw it into a nearby tree. It wrapped securely around a branch, and she climbed up the rope. She sat on the branch, leaned against the trunk, pulled a sharp knife from her pocket, and waited.

Reni was cold and wet, and the rain forest was alive with a thousand sounds. Rain dripped from bushes and trees. Reni knew that any innocent rustle could be the sound of the big cat approaching.

She pulled Grandfather's mask up over the back of her head and began to whisper. "Tiger, tiger, come to me," she chanted. Her blood ran cold when she thought of what she was doing. Alone in the dark jungle, it was easy to believe Grandfather's superstition about speaking the big cat's name.

"If I believe one old superstition, why not another?" Reni asked herself. "If it's true that I can call a tiger, it must also be true that my mask will protect me."

Reni lost track of time as she whispered the tiger's name over and over. The rain poured down twice, let up twice, and then stopped. She shivered in her soaked clothes. Water streamed off the mask and down the back of her neck, but she was too wet to care.

The tiger must have passed right beneath her, but Reni didn't hear a sound until it extended a paw and batted at the raft, making it bob in the water. In the dim light she saw the huge cat's outline. She smelled an odor that filled her with terror. Surely the cat would sense her presence and climb up after her.

Instead, the tiger gracefully leaped onto the raft and pounced on the meat. Reni grabbed the rope and slashed it with her knife.

The second she freed the raft, it spun off with the current. The tiger roared, and Reni feared it would leap to land. But in an instant, the tiger and the raft were gone.

The rest of the night was cold and lonely, but Reni managed to doze. She woke with the sun and half slid, half climbed down the sodden trunk to the ground.

She stretched her tired muscles and began the long walk home, Grandfather's mask hanging down her back. She prayed that the raft would float all the way to the National Park before it ran aground.

When she got home, she would take a nap. Then, if the weather permitted, Reni and Grandfather would wander into the forest and search for orchids.

Abbie's Light

AN ORIGINAL STORY BY TENNA LEIGH
(BASED ON A TRUE STORY)

"I will not fall. I will not fall," Abbie repeated as she clung to the pulley rope. The long, heavy rope was looped around the rims of two wheels. One wheel was attached to the storage shed near the house; the other was on a pole by the lighthouse. Papa had built the pulley system to carry buckets of oil from the shed across the rocky pathway to the light. It was also useful for keeping one's balance. The algae-covered rocks were slippery even in good weather. With a storm coming, the rising waves threw spray on the path, making it as slick as ice.

This was the very place where Mama had fallen last

week. She hadn't been holding the rope, and she'd slipped and tumbled down the jagged rocks into the sea. Luckily a fisherman had seen her fall, or she might have drowned. As it was, her left foot was torn up, and her right leg was broken.

"If Mama could walk, I wouldn't have to tend the light while Papa's away," Abbie grumbled. She was miserable. Her long skirt and petticoats were soaked and tangled around her goose-bumped legs. The wind had stolen her cape and numbed her fingers. She tugged on the rope. There was still a long way to go.

The morning had been calm and sunny when Papa left for the mainland. He had filled his small boat with lobsters and promised to be home before dark with dress cloth for Mama, a toy for baby Elizabeth, and ribbons for Abbie.

At midmorning clouds appeared on the horizon, and the wind started to blow. Only a little at first. Then worse. Then much worse. By late afternoon Abbie knew Papa would not be able to cross the rough sea. He would stay on the mainland that night, and tending the light would be up to her.

She plodded forward and tugged on the rope until the lighthouse door was within reach. Abbie pushed it open with her icy hands, unhooked the oil buckets, and lugged them inside. Her skirt caught on the door as she heaved it shut. "It's a good thing Mama sews a strong seam," she thought, "or this skirt would be in tatters now."

Inside the tower, a stairway spiraled 119 steps to the top. Abbie rested on the bottom step for a moment.

In nice weather, this island was a beautiful place to live. The blue-green ocean stretched as far as the eye could see. In the shallow water by the beach, Abbie could watch small fish darting about. Whales and dolphins circled the island, hunting for squid.

The lighthouse stood on a big flat rock that rose 15 feet above the rest of the island. Its black and white stripes and bright red roof were beautiful against a blue sky, and its windows glinted in the light. At night, its blinking light helped ships navigate the rocky coastal waters.

A sudden gust of wind pounded the lighthouse, ending Abbie's daydream. The sky was growing gloomy; soon the storm would be overhead. The light must be on before it was dark. Abbie stood up and reached for the buckets.

"Oh no," she sighed. The oil had hardened in the

cold. Now she would have to light the warming stove to melt it. And she'd better hurry.

Abbie lifted the front of her skirt and petticoats, tucked them into her apron waist so she wouldn't trip, and began the long climb. At the first landing she glanced out the window at the rough sea. There was no time to catch her breath, so up she went. At the second landing Abbie had to stop. She put the buckets down and looked toward home. The scene looked like a pencil drawing: all gray.

The rectangular stone house stood near the center of the island. At one end of the house was the chicken coop, and at the other end was the woodshed. The island was solid rock, so there was no garden, but Mama had planted geraniums in pots beneath the windows. The freshwater cistern and the storage shed were on the high ground behind the house. A fog bell stood between the house and the beach.

Abbie's heart skipped a beat. The beach was underwater, and waves were lapping at the bell. The sea was rising every second.

Abbie wanted to run back down the stairs and across the rocks. If the sea continued to rise, it would soon flood the house. Mama couldn't walk, and

Elizabeth was only three months old. But Abbie knew the light had to shine, so she pushed upward.

She didn't pause at the third landing or the fourth. At the fifth landing, a petticoat slipped from her apron. No time to tuck it up. Only two flights to go. Abbie's heart was pounding so hard, her chest hurt.

At the 112th step, the light came into view. It was over 6 feet wide and looked like a giant crystal egg. The Fresnel lens had 666 concentric glass circles held together by a gleaming brass framework. Inside the lens lay the five wicks Abbie had to light.

Abbie set one bucket on the small stove beside the lens, shoved some wood inside, and tried to light it. The pieces were too big to catch the flame. She snatched them out and replaced them with smaller sticks. Finally the fire started and the oil began to melt.

Next Abbie had to make sure the light would flash properly. Every lighthouse had a different signal, so sailors would know where they were when they saw the different lights. In order for the light to flash, the lens had to turn. It worked like a huge grandfather clock: A slowly falling weight pulled a chain over a set of gears that rotated the light. Abbie grasped the chain and hauled the weight from the floor far below.

Abbie wedged a peg in the gears so the weight wouldn't fall just yet. She grabbed the bucket, poured the oil into its chamber, and lit the wicks. Suddenly the room was filled with a light so bright it could be seen 20 miles away. "No sailors will be lost tonight," thought Abbie. She freed the weight and flew down the steps. The beacon would burn for four hours before she had to light it again.

Abbie reached the bottom step and opened the door all in one motion. She grabbed the pulley rope instinctively and hurried down the rocky path. Rain was falling so hard, she could barely see.

As Abbie reached the front door, she heard a strange, muffled clang. She whirled around and saw a wave dragging the fog bell out to sea.

"Mama, Mama!" shouted Abbie as she opened the door. "The sea is rising, and the waves are growing. I'm afraid they will flood the house. We have to get to the lighthouse! First I'll take Elizabeth, then I'll come back for you."

Abbie dashed frantically around the room, gathering warm clothes for everyone. She spread a blanket on the floor, threw the clothes on it, put the baby on top, and wrapped them all up together. She clutched the precious bundle tightly, opened the door, and saw there wasn't enough time for two trips.

"Take Elizabeth and go, Abbie! Go!" Mama shouted over the wind.

"No!" said Abbie defiantly, forcing the door shut with her hip. "I can do this, Mama. I just need to think!"

Abbie knew she could use the pulley system to help her carry the baby to safety. But Mama couldn't walk. Abbie stepped away from the door—and was stopped abruptly. Her skirt was caught in the door. Once again Mama's strong seam held up.

Strong seams . . . strong seams and . . . the pulley system! Abbie had a plan.

"Mama, hold Elizabeth while I get Papa's overalls and coat," shouted Abbie. She raced to the cupboard and grabbed the clothes. "Put on Papa's coat," she hollered, heading out the door with the overalls. "I'll be right back."

Waves washed over her feet as she struggled toward the pulley. She threw the overall straps over the rope and buttoned them. Then she tied a knot in the bottom of each leg.

As Abbie raced back to the house, she heard the chickens squawking madly in their coop. "They're terrified," she thought. Then she realized *she* wasn't afraid. Action had pushed fear aside.

"Abbie, what *are* you doing?" Mama demanded as Abbie scooped up the bundle that contained Elizabeth.

"We're all going to the lighthouse together. There's only time for one trip," she replied, running out the door again.

At the pulley, Abbie slipped Elizabeth into one leg of Papa's big overalls. She hurried to the coop, gathered the chickens in her apron, then ran back and popped them into the other leg.

Abbie raced to the house. She put her arms around Mama's chest and dragged her out the door toward the pulley. Papa's oilcloth coat made it easier. At the pulley, Abbie lifted Mama so she could grasp the rope. She carefully lifted Mama's legs and put them through the overall straps. Then she buttoned Papa's coat around the rope, making a sling that would carry Mama to safety.

But she wasn't finished yet. This storm could last for days. There was already one extra bucket of oil in the lighthouse, but she might need more. She went inside the shed and grabbed two buckets of oil and a small bag of rice. Back at the pulley, she fastened them to the rope.

Abbie made her way to the head of the parade and began to pull. It seemed to take forever. One step, then pull. Another step, pull. The heavy load made the rope sag, and Abbie had to pull hard. Left foot, pull. Right foot, pull.

Abbie was soaked to the skin by the time she reached the lighthouse. With numb fingers, she unbuttoned Papa's overalls and carried them inside. She laid Elizabeth on the floor and freed the squawking chickens. Next she dragged Mama inside, and lastly she fetched the extra supplies. Abbie shut the door, leaned against the wall, and slipped to the floor, too exhausted to even get out of her wet clothes.

Wind and waves beat at the lighthouse through the night, but it stood solid. Every four hours Abbie climbed the stairs, trimmed the wicks, and fed more oil into the light. Just after dawn, Abbie watched waves sweep her home away. But the light never wavered.

Morning didn't bring an end to the storm. It raged through that day and into the next night. Abbie collected rainwater in one of the buckets and used the little stove to cook rice and eggs. And she kept the light burning.

The third day dawned calm. As Abbie awoke, she

sensed that all was quiet—except for the footsteps she heard coming up the rocky path. Papa was back! Abbie yanked the door open, and Papa rushed inside, hugging everyone and crying with relief.

"Abbie, I'm proud of you," said Papa. "Each night I saw the light, I knew you were safe. Captain Hampton told me to tell you he was able to steer his ship safely into the harbor because your light never wavered. He'll take you all to live at his house until our new home is built. You are my shining light, Abbie."

August 25, 1857

In recognition of her outstanding bravery and dedication to duty during the great storm of February 18 and 19, 1856, during which Abbie Landis saved the lives of her family and four known ships at sea, the lighthouse formerly called Matthews Light will henceforth be known on the records of this country as

Abbie's Light

By order of the Lighthouse Board of the United States of America

Troop 13 to the Rescue

AN ORIGINAL STORY BY PENNY WARNER

"If we don't beat Troop 7 this year, I'm going to...eat a bat sandwich!" thirteen-year-old Becca Matthews announced to her three best friends as she stepped off the bus at Camp Miwok.

"How about a bat s'more?" CJ Tran planted her small feet in the red dirt of California Gold Country. "Bats taste better with chocolate."

Becca laughed. It had been a long, winding, three-hour drive from San Francisco to Camp Miwok for the scouts' Gold Rush Jamboree. Glad to get off the bus, she took a deep breath of country air—and crinkled her nose. Skunk.

"We came so close to winning the gold medal last year!" Jonnie Jackson said, twisting one of her tight black braids. "We've got to win this year. We've been preparing all month."

Becca imagined the gold medal gleaming against her own fair skin.

"Don't worry; we'll beat Troop 7," replied Sierra Garcia, Troop 13's optimist. "We've chosen our events carefully."

"I hope you're right, Sierra. After what they did to us last year—all those ants in our clothes—I couldn't stand to see them win again." Becca watched the other scouts unloading their gear and preparing their campsites. The competition looked tough, especially fourteen-year-old Tiffany Hewitt, Troop 7's oldest and tallest girl.

"Don't worry, Jonnie," CJ said. "You're so buff this year, you won't have any trouble rappelling into that cavern."

Jonnie shrugged. "I just hope those ropes hold. And what if Tiffany—"

"*Scouts!*" Susan Sanford called from the campsite. Susan had been Troop 13's leader for two years. The girls admired her businesslike ways and her warm smile—not to mention her tall, athletic build and her gorgeous brown hair.

"Girls!" Susan held up her right hand, the scout sign for quiet. Troop 13 hushed. "It's time to get to work!" Susan's words set everyone in motion. Within two hours, they had pitched their tents, stored their belongings, and lit their evening campfire.

After a meal of hot dogs and s'mores (batless), the girls sang songs and told ghost stories around the campfire. Finally it was time to hit the sleeping bags.

"Flashlights out!" Susan called. One by one the tents grew dark. Within a half-hour, Becca's tentmates were asleep.

But not Becca. She lay awake in her sleeping bag, thinking about the rappelling event that would kick off the Jamboree tomorrow. She wondered if her troop would lose the gold medal to Troop 7 again. After tossing and turning for what seemed like hours, Becca sat up. There was only one way to deal with this excess energy. She switched on her flashlight and rummaged through her backpack.

"CJ! Jonnie! Sierra! Wake up!" Becca whispered.

The three girls moaned and rolled over.

"Do you know what time it is?" Sierra yawned and checked her lighted watch.

Becca nodded. "Yeah, it's payback time." With one hand she held up a plastic baggie full of safety pins. In the other hand was a red marker.

CJ blinked. "What's that stuff for?"

Becca grinned.

Sierra and Jonnie caught on immediately and tossed back their covers.

"Oh, cool!" CJ giggled as she scrambled after her friends, who were already creeping outside. The four girls tiptoed silently among the tents in the moonlight. The smell of skunk pierced the air. Only an occasional distant howl broke the stillness.

And while Tiffany and her tentmates dreamed about winning the gold medal, the four girls from Troop 13 stood just outside the tent, unfastening the safety pins and uncapping the red marker...

"He-e-elp!"

"Get us out of here!"

"Something's after us!"

"We're trapped!"

Screams coming from one of Troop 7's tents woke

the entire camp at dawn. Girls in pajamas, nighties, and long T-shirts scrambled from their sleeping bags to see what was up.

Becca, CJ, Jonnie, and Sierra stayed put, peeking out as everyone else gathered around Tiffany's tent. Even from a distance, they could see the tent shaking as Tiffany and her friends tried to escape.

Through her binoculars Becca admired the red bull's-eye and message on the tent: "Hit the bull's-eye and win a prize!" Several girls were bombarding the target with pine cones that had been stacked conveniently nearby. Becca aimed the binoculars at the tent's door. Safety pins immobilized the three zippers. It took several minutes for the shower of pine cones and the laughter to subside so someone could undo the pins and free the four girls. All four ran for the latrine.

"I guess they had to go!" said Becca, grinning.

"Badly!" CJ agreed.

As the girls dressed for the day, they heard Tiffany yelling, "Those dorks from Troop 13 did this!"

"How'd they know it was us?" CJ whispered. Then she realized they'd been the only ones who hadn't come out to watch the fun.

Jonnie peered out the door flap. "Uh-oh," she said, "here they come."

Four girls from Troop 7 were stalking over. Tiffany wore silky pink pajamas and fluffy slippers. She had tied a sweatshirt around her waist.

Becca stepped out of the tent and stood in her holey "Girls rule!" T-shirt and sweatpants, staring at Tiffany. "What happened?" she asked. "We heard all the screaming—"

Tiffany cut Becca off. "*You* did that! You and your stupid little pals! Those dumb pine cones woke us up … and we couldn't get out to use the—to see what was going on!"

"Gosh, that's awful!" Becca said innocently.

Tiffany pulled her sweatshirt tighter around her waist. "You nimrod. We know you were behind it. That prank was just the sort of dorky thing you would do. What if we had an acci—emergency? You know the rules: Any scout who doesn't respect others is not a good scout! Trapping us in our tents is disrespectful!"

Becca tried not to laugh. "You mean like putting ants in people's clothes?"

Tiffany clenched her fists and stepped forward menacingly.

"Girls!" Susan suddenly called out. "Time to make breakfast!"

Tiffany glared at the girls from Troop 13. "We'll get you for this," she hissed. "We'll kick your butts at the rappelling competition, just like we did last year!"

As Tiffany stomped off, Becca stared at the bottom of her sweatshirt. Was that a wet spot?

"Girls! Breakfast!" Susan repeated, eyeing the girls suspiciously. They stifled their giggles and hustled to dress.

Becca thought about the upcoming event as she ate her Eggs in a Muffin. Jonnie was strong and fast, and had done lots of climbing at the gym with her parents. She'd have no trouble rappelling into the 100-foot cavern. But could she beat Tiffany?

"Did you hear about that new scout?" CJ interrupted Becca's thoughts.

Becca shrugged. "Who?"

"Amber something. She's supposed to be some kind of super-athlete. She's been bragging about being a real rock climber, not just a gym rat." CJ pointed out Amber at Troop 10's campsite.

Becca glanced over at the new girl and sized her up quickly. Amber was tall and lanky like Jonnie, with milk-chocolate skin and short, tight curls. It was hard to tell how strong she was under her baggy clothes, but it looked like Tiffany wasn't the only one Jonnie would have to beat.

"Time to go!" Susan called out. The troops hiked down the dirt path to the Haunted Caverns for the rappelling event. At the caverns, the park rangers and troop leaders checked the rappellers' harnesses, ropes, buckles, and helmets, making sure every piece of equipment was in good working order. Finally, Jonnie buckled her fanny pack over her sweatshirt.

"All right, girls," boomed Mrs. Stumplemeyer, Troop 7's leader. "You know the rules, but I'm going to review them." The girls groaned. Mrs. Stumplemeyer held up her right hand, but it was her stern look that hushed everyone.

Becca glanced over the cavern's edge. The steep cliff dropped away into a seemingly bottomless pit. She saw nothing but blackness below and shivered, thankful that this was Jonnie's event.

"When I give the command," Mrs. Stumplemeyer continued, "use your ropes to lower yourselves to the bottom of the cavern within the allotted time. If you're too slow or too fast, you'll be disqualified. We want you to rappel responsibly, not barrel down out of control. The first scout to make it to the bottom *within the time window* wins this event."

Jonnie nervously checked her watch, then stretched her muscles for the zillionth time. Becca could tell she was anxious to start.

"Hang in there," CJ said, laughing at her pun. "Get it? See you at the bottom."

The girls gave Jonnie a few more encouraging words before descending a spiral staircase to the cavern floor, where they would greet the rappellers with flashlights, cheers, and hugs as they landed.

Climbing down the staircase was almost as exciting as rappelling, Becca thought. The metal structure was shaky and dizzying. When she reached the bottom, she looked up and thought, "I'll bet they could fit the Statue of Liberty in here."

After donning the sweatshirt tied around her waist, Becca lifted her binoculars. She spotted Jonnie between Tiffany and Amber, and she waved the flashlight to signal her support. A hush fell over the crowd as the tiny figures above switched on their helmet lights.

Tweeeet! Mrs. Stumplemeyer's whistle echoed in

the cavern.

Ten girls began their descent into the blackness below, guided only by the dim flashlights of their troopmates at the bottom.

"What's happening?" Sierra asked Becca, who was still peering through the binoculars.

"Jonnie's way ahead of everyone." Becca paused. "But that new girl—Amber—she's picking up speed."

Becca shared her binoculars as the rappellers completed the first 50 feet of the descent, creeping down the cliff on their ropes like spiders trailing silk.

Becca took the binoculars from Sierra and focused them on Jonnie. Suddenly she gasped. "Oh no! Amber just passed Jonnie!" Becca's heart thumped. She searched for Tiffany and found her a few feet above Jonnie.

The other girls didn't need binoculars to see what had happened. Amber had suddenly taken the lead. No one from Troop 13 said anything, but the noise from Troop 10 grew as its members chanted, "*Am*-ber! *Am*-ber! *Am*-ber! *Am*—"

Suddenly the chanting stopped. The other spectators murmured as they realized something was wrong. Amber had stopped her descent. Becca saw it all up close through her binoculars. "Oh my gosh!

Amber's stuck! She seems to be floating in midair."

Sierra took the binoculars and studied Amber. "She's wiggling around...her rope must be caught on something."

Becca retrieved the binoculars and zeroed in on Jonnie, who had almost caught up with Amber. Tiffany was right behind Jonnie. The other rappellers had stopped descending to watch Amber, who was squirming frantically.

Becca trained her binoculars on Amber. "She's definitely caught on something; it looks like a rough ledge sticking out of the cliff. Her rope...," Becca paused, straining to make out what Amber was doing. "She's trying to get free...but every time she wiggles around, the rope rubs against that ledge and...oh no..."

"What?!" CJ shouted.

"...it's...fraying."

A hush fell over the crowd as everyone realized the danger Amber was in. The sharp edge of the jutting ledge was sawing away at her lifeline.

Becca aimed the binoculars at Jonnie again. "Uh-oh."

"What now?" CJ grabbed at the binoculars, but Becca held on.

"Something's wrong with Jonnie now. She's

slowing down," Becca said.

"Oh no!" Sierra asked. "Is she stuck, too?"

"I can't tell, but she's definitely stopped." Becca gasped. "She's…trying to reach Amber!"

The three girls looked at each other. "But what about the contest?" CJ said. "Tiffany's almost caught up with her!"

If Jonnie continued her descent now, she would win the rappelling event. But instead she had stopped abruptly. Becca watched through the binoculars as Jonnie began swinging her legs back and forth.

Becca moved her gaze to Tiffany and saw the girl pause for a moment as she reached Jonnie and Amber. Jonnie, still swinging her legs, said something over her shoulder to Tiffany, but Becca couldn't make out the words over the spectators' concerned chatter. Tiffany didn't seem to hear Jonnie either. Or she'd chosen to ignore her. She slid past Jonnie and Amber, continuing her descent.

Tiffany had taken the lead.

The murmuring increased as Troop 7 watched their teammate rappel toward the bottom of the cavern and victory. Becca kept her eyes on Jonnie, who continued swinging her legs, trying to reach

Amber. Amber looked terrified as she squirmed around, trying to free herself.

"Oh no!" Becca whispered.

"What?" CJ squealed.

"The rope…another strand is about to—"

The strand broke before Becca could finish her sentence. Amber jerked downward a foot. She screamed, and so did the girls at the bottom of the cavern.

Becca focused on Jonnie. "Come on, Jonnie, come on!" she murmured. Jonnie spent several more seconds kicking her legs as she swung back and forth, trying to gain momentum. Becca could see Amber crying as she reached out for Jonnie, who swung only 2 feet away from her.

With one more vigorous kick, Jonnie was able to grab Amber's outstretched arm. Amber threw her arms around Jonnie like a lost toddler who'd just found her mother.

Gripping Amber with one hand, Jonnie found a foothold on the cliff and struggled out of her sweatshirt. She wrapped it around Amber's waist and her own, tying the sleeves tightly with a knot she'd learned for her camping badge. Then Jonnie opened her fanny pack and pulled out her metal flashlight.

She lifted it high in the air and slammed it against the sharp, thin edge of the ledge. Becca watched the rocky tip break off and fall to the ground.

Amber jerked as her rope was freed, but she clung to Jonnie, and the sweatshirt held them tightly together. Together, with one strong rope and one frayed nearly in half, the two girls slowly started to descend.

"She's free!" A cheer went up from the cavern floor. The girls hugged each other, and leaders wiped sweat from their foreheads. Everyone was happy to see that Amber was out of danger. Soon the girls were only 5 or 6 feet from the ground.

And then Amber's rope snapped completely. Jonnie's rope couldn't handle the jolt of extra weight, and the girls plummeted the last few feet.

They landed hard enough to knock the wind out of them. As they gasped and coughed, their troopmates gathered around them and helped them to their feet. It was clear from the cheers that both Amber and Jonnie were going to be all right.

But the members of Troop 7 were cheering for a different reason. Tiffany had landed at the bottom several minutes before Amber and Jonnie. Troop 7 had won the rappelling event.

"Losers!" Tiffany sneered at Troop 13. "I told you we were going to beat you this year!"

Becca shook her head, then turned to help Jonnie remove her gear. Jonnie didn't look so good. "Are you all right?" Becca said as she unhooked one of Jonnie's ropes. "You were amazing!"

"But we lost the event again," Jonnie protested, "thanks to me."

"Jonnie!" CJ said. "You did the right thing. You saved Amber's life. And you risked your life to do it!"

Sierra chimed in, "I thought what you did was great. So what if we didn't win? That's not the point."

"The girls are right, Jonnie," came a voice from the darkness. Susan stepped forward, holding her flashlight. "You're a scout, and that means you help others when they're in trouble. I'm very proud of you." Susan put her arm around Jonnie and gave her a squeeze. Jonnie's look of disappointment faded a little.

Becca glanced over at Tiffany, who was accepting congratulations from her circle of friends. "I just wish Troop 7 hadn't won. They're driving us nuts with all their bragging."

"Scouts! Sco-o-u-uts!" Mrs. Stumplemeyer's shrill voice echoed like a siren in the cavern. "We have our winner! I'm pleased to announce that thanks to Tiffany Hewitt, Troop 7 has won the rappelling event."

A brief spurt of applause followed. It came mostly from Troop 7.

"Yes, Mrs. Stumplemeyer," said another voice in the darkness. It was Mrs. Parker, the leader of Troop 10— Amber's troop. She stepped forward, followed by several other troop leaders. "Troop 7 won the event. But we have another award to present."

"What do you mean, another award?" snapped Mrs. Stumplemeyer. "There's only one winner for the rappelling event. I don't see—"

Mrs. Parker interrupted, "It's great to be a winner. But it's even better to be a good scout—"

Mrs. Stumplemeyer broke in, "What do you mean? My girls are good scouts."

"Mrs. Stumplemeyer, you didn't let me finish. I was about to say that Amber was in serious danger up there, and a scout from another troop forfeited the race to rescue her. This is a stellar demonstration of the Scout Promise, 'To help other people at all times.'"

"So?" said Mrs. Stumplemeyer, puzzled.

"So, while your troop has won the rappelling event," Mrs. Parker continued, "the other troop leaders and I believe that Jonnie Jackson from Troop 13 deserves an even higher honor—one of the highest honors a scout can receive: the Leadership Pin. She clearly gave up her winning edge to help Amber, and she has set a fine example for everyone."

"Yes, but—"

"This type of behavior should be rewarded, not punished. Don't you agree, Mrs. Stumplemeyer?"

Troop 7's leader glanced at her scouts, then nodded weakly.

"Shall we take a vote?" asked Mrs. Parker. "All in favor that Jonnie Jackson from Troop 13 be awarded the Leadership Pin, raise your hands." Ninety percent of the hands went up. "Those opposed?" Several hands from Troop 7 started to go up, then faltered. Only one hand stayed up: Tiffany's.

Tiffany looked around with disgust. "It's not fair!" she whined. "You're just trying to downplay my award by giving her a better one! What about that trick they played on us this morning! *That* wasn't setting a good example!"

Susan stepped forward and stood face to face with Tiffany. "My girls didn't complain when you put their clothes on an anthill last year."

Tiffany muttered and stomped off. As a crowd gathered around Jonnie to congratulate her, Becca stood back, smiling at Susan. It looked as if one good deed had led to another. Troop 7 may have won the first event, but Troop 13 had won an even higher honor by doing the right thing. Becca glanced over at the girls in Troop 7, who were huddled tightly and whispering.

"I wonder what they're up to," Sierra said to Becca.

"I don't know," Becca replied, "but I think we'd better zip up our tents tight tonight!"

Dear Reader: If you enjoyed this story, you will also like the novel based on it, *The Mystery of the Haunted Caves*. Look for it in your bookstore starting in July 2001.

The Treasure beneath the Hay

An Original Story by Nancy Alpert Mower

Russian Word:

Cossacks: a group of people from Russia who were famous for their skill on horseback.

Dust in her eyes. Mud on her pinafore. This trip was not fun.

Goldie sat on top of the hay, her hands folded in her lap. Her six-year-old sister, Lizabeta, crawled about the wagon. Lizabeta didn't understand how serious this journey was. Goldie, who was nine, understood it well. She knew that she and Lizabeta must guard the treasure hidden beneath the hay.

Papa sat on a wooden plank at the front of the wagon, driving the family's horse. Mama sat quietly beside him, her long gray skirt folded around her legs. A black shawl rested lightly on her shoulders.

As the wagon clattered along the narrow, dusty road, grit flew into Goldie's nose and eyes. When the horse came to a puddle, he clopped right through it, splattering Goldie's pinafore with brown mud.

Goldie didn't want to be sitting on a pile of scratchy hay, rattling over a bumpy road in this rickety old wagon. She wished she were back home in Odessa, helping her mother in the house and her father in the tannery, and playing in the little yard when the day's work was finished. But someone else now lived in the house. Some other people now ran the tannery. Goldie and her family were leaving Russia, and she knew she would probably never see home again.

First they were going to a cousin's wedding in Romania. Then they would head for the Black Sea, where they would board a ship and travel many weeks until they reached another country called the United States. Goldie didn't want to go to the United States. People there spoke a strange language called English that she was sure she'd never understand. Living in a new country would be hard, and getting out of their old country would not be easy, either. Goldie had heard the grownups talking about it back in Odessa.

Grandmama had said, "I tell you, 1888 is not a good year to try to leave this country."

"At any moment you could be stopped by soldiers," Grandpapa had added.

"And that would be a disaster," her uncle had insisted. "Your only hope would be to bribe them." Goldie wasn't sure what it meant to bribe people, but from the way her uncle sounded, she knew it wasn't good.

Papa, however, was determined to leave the country. "We know we're taking a risk," he said. "But it's worth it if we can save our treasure."

Our treasure. Our treasure. Goldie was tired of hearing all this talk about treasure. The treasure was only her two little brothers, four-year-old Ivan and two-year-old Aleksei. That's what was hidden beneath the hay, out of Russian soldiers' sight. It was all because her family was Jewish. Papa and Mama had explained it to Goldie.

"When Jewish boys are eight years old, they are drafted into the Russian army," Papa told her.

"That's not a good thing." Mama wiped tears from her eyes as she spoke.

"Not good at all," said Papa. "Because Jewish boys are usually the first ones sent to the front lines in battle. And soldiers in the front lines are usually the first ones to get killed."

Goldie certainly didn't want Ivan and Aleksei to get killed. She really loved her little brothers. But she thought people worried about them too much. After all, such young boys would probably adjust easily to life in a new country. But she and Lizabeta had to leave their friends and their way of life and start all over. No one seemed to care about that. Everyone just talked about the danger they would be in if the Russians found her family trying to sneak two little boys out of the country.

Tears welled up in Goldie's eyes as she remembered saying good-bye to her friends and relatives. She remembered exactly how it felt to hug her grandmother for the last time. Bending down a little, Grandmama had rested her cheek against Goldie's. "You're the oldest, Goldela," Grandmama had said. "We're all counting on you to help save the treasure."

"How can I do that?" Goldie had asked. "I don't

know how to save anyone."

"You'll know when the time comes," Grandmama had told her. "Remember that you were born with three special gifts. You have sharp senses, a stout heart, and a keen mind. Use them well, and you will be all right."

Goldie had no idea how she could use her senses, her heart, or her mind to keep her brothers safe. But she loved her grandmother very much, so she had squeezed her and said, "I'll remember, Grandmama."

Goldie's family had left Odessa three days ago, traveling from sunup to sundown. Every night Papa steered the wagon off the road to a sheltered spot. They all ate some of the food Mama had packed and then slept on the hay. At first light each morning, they tucked the two little boys under the hay and continued on their journey.

Papa had said it would probably take four days to get out of the country. Hopefully this would be their last day in Russia. So far no one had bothered them. And so far the boys had been fairly quiet. But Goldie worried about what she would do if her brothers started making noise.

At that moment she heard Aleksei whimpering and sobbing under the hay. She spoke to him softly. "It's all right, little one. I'm here to look after you." She forced herself to keep her voice calm. If Aleksei sensed her fear, he would cry even louder. Quietly, Goldie sang a lilting lullaby. Gradually the whimpering stopped. Aleksei must have gone back to sleep. Lizabeta slept, too, lying beside Goldie on top of the hay.

Goldie groped through the scratchy hay and touched Aleksei's shoulder. She rested her hand on his chest and felt the soft rise and fall of his breathing. Then she moved over and felt for Ivan. He was asleep, too. Goldie groped around in the hay a bit more. She felt the stack of newly made leather gloves and remembered spending many days and evenings helping her parents stitch them.

A few of the gloves were wedding presents. But most would come along to the new country. Papa had said, "We can sell or trade them to help us get started." There were other leather goods beneath the hay, too: some vests and a handsome jacket worth a lot of money. The leather goods would buy food and shelter until Papa could find a job.

Goldie let her fingers linger a moment on the smooth leather. Then she pulled her arm out of the hay and once again folded her hands in her lap. The only sounds were the twittering of birds, the *clip-clop* of the horse, and the rattling of the wagon. But—wait a minute—those were not the only sounds.

Goldie's sharp ears picked up a distant clatter. It sounded like horses trotting through the woods. Trotting horses could mean only one thing: soldiers! They were still far away, but the sounds were slowly getting louder. Goldie remembered Papa's bad ear infection last winter. He had lost some of his hearing and probably didn't notice the faint noise of the soldiers. She must warn him! Leaning forward, she whispered, "Papa, there are soldiers in the woods. Off to the right."

Papa reined the horse to an abrupt halt. He listened. "You're right. I hear them now. We must hide."

Pulling the horse toward the left, he drove off the road and into the woods. The trees here were so thick, sunlight barely filtered through the branches. Papa kept driving through the dim woods until he could no longer see the road. Then he stopped.

"Clever Papa," Goldie thought. "If we can't see the road, people on the road can't see us." Lizabeta woke up and started to ask a question. Goldie shushed her by putting a finger to her own lips and a finger over her sister's mouth. It was important for her family to be perfectly silent. Even a tiny noise could attract the soldiers' attention.

The sound of horses was louder now and accompanied by men's voices. Goldie could tell that the soldiers were coming out of the woods. They galloped down the road, gaily shouting to one another. Goldie held her breath and prayed her little brothers would not wake up. More shouting soldiers came out of the woods. Goldie sat still as stone, barely breathing, as the horses clattered along the lane.

In a few minutes all the soldiers had passed. Papa waited a few more minutes. Then he drove the wagon out of the woods and back onto the road. "Good work, Goldela," he praised her warmly. "Your warning helped save our treasure."

Papa's praise made Goldie feel cozy and happy. It was good to know she had used her sharp sense of hearing wisely. She'd helped her family along their journey to the United States. Still, she wished they were home in Odessa.

All was quiet again. The horse plodded along, and the boys slept. Goldie and Lizabeta talked softly. "What would happen if the soldiers saw us?" Lizabeta asked.

Goldie tried to remember what the grownups had said back in Odessa. "Grandpapa said we'll probably be all right as long as the Russians don't discover the boys," she told her sister.

"But what if they do?" Lizabeta asked.

"Uncle Yuri said the soldiers might take the boys. They would probably send the rest of us home." This was the first time Goldie had let herself speak those horrible words aloud. Now she truly understood how important it was that the boys stay hidden. Although they were rascals sometimes, she could not imagine living without them. She realized that she had been selfish to fret about leaving her friends. Keeping the whole family together was much more important. But still, she would so much rather be safe at home in Odessa than out here in the woods, facing her fears.

The girls sat silently, each lost in her own thoughts, as the horse plodded onward. Goldie noticed that the trees beside the road were thinning out. The wagon was nearing the edge of the woods. They passed fewer and fewer trees, until finally they rolled out onto thick, green pastureland. Every now and then they passed a stately farmhouse, but the houses were far apart.

After the family had crossed a few miles of open

pastureland, Goldie again heard the clatter of horses' hoofs. Soldiers were behind the little wagon, approaching rapidly. Here there were no woods to hide in. If they all kept quiet, maybe the soldiers would pass them by.

But as the Russians came near, Ivan sneezed. "The noise probably woke him," Goldie thought, "and some hay dust tickled his nose." Ivan kept sneezing as the soldiers rode closer and closer. Goldie could not shush him! She dared not be seen speaking into the hay. Now Aleksei was awake, too. Goldie could hear his baby voice clearly.

She nearly froze with fear as the soldiers drew alongside the wagon. Then suddenly she knew what she must do. She said loudly, "Come on, Liza, let's sing. Remember that song about the Cossacks?" It was a long, rollicking ballad Uncle Yuri had taught them last winter. Elbowing Lizabeta in the ribs, Goldie whispered, "Sing with me—as loud as you can."

People had always complimented Goldie on her soft voice and her good manners. She didn't like behaving so rudely. But she knew she had to do this. At the top of their lungs, the girls sang to drown out the sounds coming from beneath the hay.

The soldiers ordered Papa to stop the wagon. Goldie and Lizabeta kept on singing. As she sang, Goldie strained to hear the grownups talking. "Those are pretty noisy children you got there," one soldier said.

"I'm sorry," said Papa. "But they love to sing."

Another soldier looked disdainfully at Papa's long hair and beard, then said, "You people are Jewish, aren't you?"

"Yes, we are," Mama replied quietly.

Goldie and Lizabeta kept singing loudly.

The first soldier barked, "Are your children always such brats?"

"I apologize for my naughty daughters," Mama said.

"Well, what can you expect from Jews?" The soldiers laughed. Then they rode away.

Goldie knew Mama and Papa were secretly proud of her. She knew it took a stout heart to keep singing in front of Russian soldiers. But she didn't like being called a brat, and she didn't like being in constant danger. Maybe now Papa would realize that this trip wasn't a good idea. It was too risky. Maybe now he would turn the wagon around and head back to Odessa.

No such luck.

Papa continued to drive the horse straight ahead.

Aleksei and Ivan were talking to each other. Goldie spoke softly into the hay. "Listen, you two: I know it's hard, but you've got to keep quiet. This is the last day you'll have to travel under the hay. But today you must not make any more noise. No sneezing. No talking. No crying. Do you understand?"

The boys didn't answer. Apparently they understood.

Goldie noticed that the farmhouses were now clustered closer together. The road widened enough for two wagons to pass. Soon the road was lined with stores and houses. Papa turned his head and told the girls, "We just have to pass through this little town, and then we'll reach the border."

It seemed to take hours to ride through the town, which was teeming with men, women, and children on foot and on horseback. Finally the road ended near a group of brown buildings. Soldiers marched in the yard in front of the buildings. This must be the border.

"Sit up now," Goldie said to Lizabeta, who was lying on the hay.

"Will we have to sing again?" Lizabeta asked, as she sat up.

"Probably not. I think the boys got the message; they're quiet now." Both girls folded their hands primly in their laps.

The wagon had reached a tall wooden fence with a locked gate. Soldiers with swords stood on each side of the gate. Other armed soldiers ran toward the wagon. The one in front had two rows of shining medals on his jacket. Goldie thought he was the captain.

"Just where do you think you're going?" the captain asked Papa.

"We're traveling into Romania to my cousin's wedding," Papa said.

"And do you have papers?" the captain growled.

Papa reached beneath his seat and pulled out a pouch of papers. The captain silently looked them over. Then he handed the papers to another soldier and strolled toward the back of the wagon saying, "And what do you have here?"

"These are my two daughters," Papa answered quietly. Goldie didn't know how Papa could keep his voice so calm. She was so frightened she felt cold, but she willed herself not to shiver. She sat stiller than she had ever sat before.

The captain glowered at Goldie and Lizabeta. He gripped Goldie by the shoulder, then patted her back. "This one feels healthy enough," he said.

Then, as Goldie watched in horror, the captain reached into the hay. "And what have we under here?" he asked.

Goldie couldn't let the soldier see her fear. What could she do? She had to think fast.

Quickly, she reached into the hay with both hands down. "Oh no, Papa," she said. "The soldiers have discovered the treasure." With one hand she lifted out the leather jacket, and with the other a stack of gloves. "I'm sorry, Papa," she said. "I know these were to be wedding gifts, but I think we'd better give them to the soldiers."

The captain pulled his hand out of the hay and took the leather goods from Goldie. He stared at the gloves and ran his fingers up and down the jacket. Goldie held her breath. Everyone in the wagon was silent.

The captain examined the leather goods for a long time. Finally he spoke. "This is very fine leather. It will do nicely, thank you." He nodded to his aide, and the soldier gave the papers back to Papa. "You have permission to cross the border. Enjoy the wedding."

Now Goldie remembered what Uncle Yuri had said about bribing. That's just what she had done. Perhaps it wasn't good to bribe, but it had been necessary to save her brothers.

A soldier opened the gate, and Papa drove the wagon through. The sun was setting; it would soon be dark. The family rode in silence for several miles. Then Papa stopped the horse. He and Mama climbed down from their seat. Goldie and Lizabeta jumped off the hay. Papa reached into the hay for Ivan and Aleksei. "Come, my treasures," he said. "We are free."

While Papa was lifting the boys out, Mama wrapped one arm around Goldie and the other around Lizabeta. "You were wonderful," she told Goldie. "You really saved us." As Goldie kissed her mother, she felt tears on Mama's cheeks. Goldie knew Mama was happy, but she suddenly realized that Mama probably also felt sad about leaving her friends and family in Odessa. Goldie had been so wrapped up in self-pity that she hadn't even thought about Mama's feelings. She wrapped both arms around Mama and hugged her.

Papa was whirling around with Ivan and Aleksei in his arms, singing, "We're free! We're free!"

Then he set the boys down, walked over to Goldie, and put his arms around her shoulders. "See your big sister here?" he said to his sons. "When you are older, in the new country, I want you to remember it's this sister you have to thank. It was Goldie, with her sharp ears, her brave heart, and her keen mind, who made it possible for all of us to go together to the United States."

Mama was smiling gently at Goldie. Goldie smiled back. Maybe living in the United States would not be so bad. At least the family would all be together. After the wedding, they would sail across the ocean. And even though they didn't have much leather left to sell, their real treasure was alive and well.

Firedance

AN ORIGINAL STORY BY BONNIE BRIGHTMAN

Spanish Words:

Dos: two

El Jefe (pronounced "el HEF-ay"): the boss.

Mesa (pronounced "MAY-sa"): literally, a table. Also used to describe a big hill with a flat top.

¡Mis niños! ¡Gracias a Dios! (pronounced "mees NEE-nyos! GRAH-syus ah DYOS!"): My children! Thank God!

Piñata (pronounced "peen-YAH-tuh"): decorated hanging container filled with candies or toys.

Sí (pronounced "see"): yes

Tres (pronounced "trace"): three

Uno: one

Angelita was worried. She sat on the steps of the trailer, watching the sun begin its slow descent behind the mesa. She knew there was a fire up on that big hill. She could smell the smoke, taste it in her mouth, and feel it in her throat. But she couldn't see it.

The trailer sat on the plain at the base of the mesa. If the fire reached the edge of the flat-topped mesa, it would roar down the hillside, feeding on the dry bitterbrush and sage that grew there. At the bottom of the mesa, it would burn even faster through the parched cheatgrass that covered the plain.

Why was Mama taking so long to fetch the medicine for Chichi's earache? Angelita sighed as she looked out at all the work her family had done. There was the well that Papa and two men from the migrant council had dug, its precious water springing up cool and clear. There was the shed for Lupita, the family's goat. Angelita and her younger brother, Chichi, had helped Papa build the shed at night after he got home from work. They had painted it pink with pretty green trim. Next to that they had built a pen for their three hens, Uno, Dos, and Tres. Their rooster, El Jefe, would perch on one of the fence posts for hours, guarding everything in sight.

Together the family had planted the garden spreading out from the foot of the steps. It was full of corn, beans—whatever they could get seeds for—to help feed the family through the winter. In one corner grew Papa's hot peppers, each with its own hot name: Blasting Cap, Last Gasp, Third Rail, Lightning Bolt, and his favorite, Firedance. Papa had created Firedance himself by carefully crossbreeding other varieties. It was the hottest pepper of all.

"*¡Ah, que linda!* How beautiful!" Papa would say as he tended his special peppers. "Have you ever seen such a pepper, Angelita?"

"No, Papa," Angelita always answered, even though she didn't really like *any* kind of hot pepper. Papa was so pleased with Firedance.

Angelita got up and walked to the other side of the trailer. A mile off to the east, she could just see Black Cat Road running parallel to the mesa. During last year's growing season, Papa had waited out there every morning before dawn for the migrant workers' truck to take him to the fields near town. When school started in the fall, the whole family walked out to the road. A school bus came for Angelita and Chichi, and Mama went with Papa to pick fruits and vegetables.

For the first time last winter, they did not go south with the other migrant workers to look for work.

Instead, the family bought the trailer and 3 acres of land with money they'd saved. Papa proudly announced that they were home now. They would never have to live in the poor conditions of the migrant camps again.

Through the winter Papa did odd jobs for the growers, and Mama cleaned other people's houses. When the growing season started again, Papa went back to work in the fields. Soon the family had almost enough money to fill the *piñata* they had brought from Mexico. The piñata was for Angelita's tenth birthday later in the summer. The money was for their future.

The sun beat down on Angelita as she thought about what fire could do to that future. There was still no smoke to be seen on the mesa, but the smell was getting stronger. What could be keeping Mama? Maybe she'd had trouble getting a ride back from town.

Angelita knew how destructive a brushfire wildfire could be. Just a month ago, the family had watched fire trucks from town hurtling off Black Cat Road toward a fire to the south. A great cloud of dust had mingled with the smoke blowing north toward the trailer.

After the firefighters were finished, Angelita and Chichi had climbed up the mesa. From the top, they could see that the fire had eaten up hundreds of acres of rangeland, jumping irrigation ditches and burning everything in its path. It had stopped right at the southeastern edge of the family's property. "It looks like a big piece of burned toast," Chichi had said. "There's nothing left!"

If this new fire came down the side of the mesa, Angelita knew she couldn't do much to protect her home. Pushed by the wind, the fire would fan out at the foot of the mesa. There wouldn't even be time to run. If they left now, maybe they could make it to the road and meet Mama on her way home. Angelita ran back around the trailer, up the steps, and inside.

"Chichi," she said gently, "get up. I know you feel sick, but we have to go on a little trip."

Chichi sat up and rubbed his ear. "Without Mama?"

"Yes, without Mama," Angelita said, pulling a shirt on over his head. "Find your hat, let's go."

Angelita put on her own wide-brimmed hat. She went to the sink and filled a jug with water. She grabbed a plastic bag from the counter and filled it with cheese and apples. She saw a box of crackers in the cabinet and tossed it in, too. Then she took two cups and a couple of pots from the cupboard.

Next she pulled the blanket off her parents' bed, rolled it up hastily, and looked for the flashlight.

"Chichi," she said, "pick one thing to take with you. We might not be coming back."

Chichi stared at his sister. Then he walked over and picked up the piñata full of money.

She smiled in spite of herself, then went outside and put everything in the big, battered wagon that one of the growers had given Chichi. Papa had replaced the wheels and added plenty of grease. Now the old wagon pulled as smooth as silk.

"Chichi," Angelita yelled, "get the hens in the crate if you can!" She grabbed a rag from the shed, wet it with the hose, and ran to the garden. She carefully dug up three of Papa's plants, gently wrapped them in the rag, and brought them back to the wagon.

Then she aimed the hose at the wooden steps and soaked them down. Maybe the metal sides of the trailer wouldn't burn as easily. She didn't dare take the time to soak the shed.

Lupita was prancing nervously about. "Come on, Lupita," Angelita urged soothingly, leading the goat to the back of the wagon and tying her there.

"Good boy, Chichi," Angelita said when she saw

Uno, Dos, and Tres settled cozily in their crate. Together they lifted the crate onto the wagon. El Jefe flew up and sat on top.

Angelita pulled the wagon, and Chichi walked beside her. "Where are we going?" he asked.

"Out to the road. We'll wait for Mama there," Angelita said calmly. She didn't want Chichi to see her fear.

But as they approached the road, Angelita could see no sign of Mama. There were no cars or trucks in the distance, either. She glanced over her shoulder and saw black smoke rising from the top of the mesa. She stopped in her tracks. If no cars came by, she and Chichi would be in big trouble on the road. Even if they crossed the road, they would not be safe. If a wildfire could jump an irrigation ditch, it could jump a road, too.

Angelita turned abruptly and headed back toward the trailer, causing Lupita to yank her head in protest. The hens fluttered and squawked, and El Jefe hopped madly about on top of the crate.

"Angelita! The fire! We can't go back that way!" Chichi yelled.

"We have to!" she insisted, knowing that their lives

depended on it. A fire needed fuel, and there was only one place without any: the Piece of Toast.

El Jefe jumped off the crate and scurried back toward the road. Chichi scooped him up, clamped him firmly under his arm, and followed his sister obediently. "Look, Angelita!" he cried suddenly, pointing at the mesa.

Angelita looked up and saw fire streaking down the hillside of the mesa. They sprinted back across the plain toward the Piece of Toast. They saw flames heading for the trailer, but soon everything was concealed by smoke. Angelita and Chichi put their heads down and ran on. There was little time.

"Chichi!" Angelita gasped, "try to keep the crate from bouncing off the wagon!" Chichi used his free hand to steady the crate. The smoke stung their eyes and throats. Ash caught in their hair and clothing. Angelita stopped for an instant to wet a handkerchief and tie it over her brother's mouth. She said, "This will help with the smoke." She was pretty sure they could survive the smoke if they kept low. But they must get far onto the Piece of Toast to survive the fire.

They kept on running when they reached the Piece of Toast, until Chichi stumbled and could go no farther. Angelita sat on the ground, holding on to him with one hand and the wagon with the other. She stayed that way long after the fire had burned its way to the road and beyond.

As night settled, Angelita looked gratefully at the charred ground. In the moonlight, she could see a few "fire followers," the tiny wildflowers that grew out of the ashes of fires on the desert plains. They were reminders that life had a way of bouncing back from destruction.

Chichi stirred and looked up at Angelita. "How's your ear?" she asked, feeling his forehead with her hand.

"Okay," he said. "Now what do we do?"

"We're camping out," she said cheerfully, knowing this would please him and send him into action.

They untied Lupita and lifted the hens' crate off the wagon. Angelita tipped the wagon on its side, so it would provide shelter from the wind. Chichi draped the blanket over the wagon and anchored the corners with shoes to create a makeshift tent.

"Come on, Lupita," Angelita murmured, setting one of the pots under the goat. As the smoke had lessened, Lupita had relaxed. She stood patiently as Angelita milked her. Angelita carefully set the milk by the wagon. She let the hens out of their crate, scattered cracker bits on the ground for them, and put some water in the other pot for them.

The cool night air was drawing moisture down toward the earth, causing the fire off in the distance to "lie down" and smolder. Its hot spots would flare up again in tomorrow's sunshine, but for now it was quiet.

"Everything is going to be okay," Angelita decided. She sat down next to Chichi and wearily bit into an apple. Suddenly a soft growl broke through the stillness, reawakening her fear. Angelita and Chichi were not the only creatures who'd sought refuge on the Piece of Toast. The chunk of apple stuck in Angelita's throat when she saw the amber eyes of a coyote gleaming in the dark.

"Chichi! The hens! Get them back in the crate!" Angelita whispered raspily. She fished about furiously for a weapon. The coyote settled gracefully on its haunches, ready to spring. Suddenly Angelita's hand closed around the pot handle. She drew her arm back and flung the pot directly at those gleaming eyes.

Clang! Yelp! The coyote turned and ran, looking back at Angelita one last time. Angelita spun around and saw Chichi scurrying after the hens. She caught the end of Lupita's rope just as the frightened goat started to bolt away into the darkness.

"Are you scared, Angelita?" Chichi whispered later, as he peeked out of the makeshift tent at his sister. Angelita was sitting on guard, leaning back against Lupita, who rested on the ground next to the tent. The hens were clucking in their crate, while El Jefe paced about nervously.

"I'm okay, Chichi. Go to sleep," she said quietly. She didn't feel okay, though. She shone the flashlight into the darkness, knowing the coyote—and maybe worse—was out there somewhere. "Well, if he comes back, he'll leave with another lump on his head," she thought, making sure she could reach a pot if necessary.

Angelita was milking Lupita at dawn when she heard the drone of an airplane overhead. It was probably headed toward the fire, dropping chemicals on the hot spots until the fire crew could smother them one by one with dirt.

Chichi crawled out of the tent to look at the plane and wave. A half-hour later, a yellow truck came speeding toward them from the direction of the fire. As it got closer, the children saw Papa leaning out the window of the passenger seat. The truck had barely stopped when he jumped out and gathered them in his arms.

"*¡Mis niños! ¡Gracias a Dios!*" he cried, his eyes toward the sky.

"Is the fire out, Papa?" Angelita asked. She was afraid to ask about the trailer.

"*Sí,*" Papa said. "It's out. It burned the shed and the garden—and the ground all around. But the trailer's still there! It's damaged, but it's still there."

The driver helped Papa load the animals and other things in the back of the truck. Angelita climbed up with Lupita to keep her calm. Chichi, holding fast to the piñata that contained the family's savings, sat next to Papa in the front seat. Only El Jefe refused to get in the truck.

"*¡No se preocupen por él!* Don't worry about him!" laughed Papa. "He'll get home on his own."

That evening, the family sat next to the charred steps of their trailer and began to plan. It was getting late in the growing season, but they could try replanting the garden. Papa would rebuild the shed this weekend. They would replace the heat-cracked windows and wash the ash off the sides of the trailer. The fire had come right up the steps before it had whirled away toward the road.

"You know, Angelita," Papa said somberly, "if you had not left the trailer when you did—"

"We have much to be thankful for," Mama broke in happily. "And we got the medicine into Chichi at last!" She hugged her children close.

"Oh Papa, I forgot!" Angelita cried, jumping up and running to get the plastic bag she'd packed yesterday. She reached in carefully and drew out three limp pepper plants.

"Firedance!" Papa exclaimed, holding the plants gently in his hand. "You even saved Firedance!"

Angelita woke in the morning to the sound of El Jefe crowing at the rising sun. She lay in her bed and smiled. It was good to be home.

Taneya's Best Shot

An Original Story by Debra Tracy

Taneya sat with her back against the bamboo wall of her family's hut, hugging her knees to her chest. She heard the door creak open and turned to see her father step outside.

"Why the long face, Taneya?" Father asked. "Jason will be back in a few weeks." Jason was a Peace Corps volunteer who helped Taneya's father patrol the Rwandan rain forest for poachers. He was visiting his family in America.

"I don't have anybody to play basketball with," she pouted. Jason had rigged up a wire hoop and hung it on the outside of the hut. Taneya had watched in open-mouthed delight as he dribbled the ball and shot it through the hoop. Then Jason taught her how to play. *Thud! Thud! Thud!* The noise nearly drove her parents crazy.

Father frowned regretfully. He was a ranger at Volcanoes National Park. His job was to protect the animals in the rain forest. Most evenings he returned home after dark and was too tired to shoot baskets with Taneya.

"I'm sorry for complaining, Father."

He smiled. "I'll tell you what: With Jason gone, I need help watching over the animals. If you can find someone to join me on my rounds today, I might have time to play basketball with you later."

Taneya's eager smile almost dispersed the low gray clouds veiling the rain forest. "Are you going to visit the gorillas?" she asked.

Father nodded. "I'm going to check on group three. Winna should have had her baby by now."

"I know just the person!" Taneya squealed, jumping up and bounding through the door. She slipped out of her yellow skirt and tugged on a pair of pants, leaving on her blouse and orange head tie.

Then she wiggled into a pair of sneakers and jogged to Father's Land Rover.

"Will any tourists be out today?" Taneya asked as Father shifted the Land Rover into gear and headed down the rutted service road.

Father shook his head.

Taneya smiled contentedly. She tried not to be selfish about the mountain gorillas. Tourists came from all over the world to visit them, and Rwanda needed the tourists' money. Still, Taneya was happiest when she and her father had the gorillas and the rain forest to themselves.

Father stopped the Land Rover a half-mile from a dense grove of bamboo called the bamboo zone. It was the gorillas' favorite feeding place.

"Poacher activity has been heavy lately," he told Taneya. "Watch for snares when you walk through the zone."

Side by side, they threaded their way through the tall bamboo, their eyes scanning for any stem bent to the ground by a rope. The rope would be slipknotted and attached to a trigger. When an animal stepped into the noose, it would tighten around the animal's limb and jerk it off the ground to dangle there until a poacher found it. The poacher would then sell the animal—or parts of it. Taneya had been disgusted to hear that someone would actually buy a gorilla hand to use as an ashtray or elephant tusks to make jewelry. A person could step into a snare, too. Father had warned Taneya to avoid the bamboo zone when she was alone.

Beyond the zone, Father and Taneya trekked deeper into group three's 10-square-mile territory. They cautiously approached a meadow where the gorillas liked to lounge on sunny days. It was drizzling now. Father led Taneya to a spot where tangled vines formed an umbrella overhead. He used a machete to cut a trail through the thick underbrush.

Taneya tugged on Father's shirt and pointed. "Look, Nuru's up in that tree." Nuru was Winna's son, a four-year-old juvenile gorilla.

"Naoom! Naoom!" Father sang out. If Father and Taneya surprised the gorillas, they might charge—or even attack.

Sultan, the 400-pound silver-backed leader, walked over on his feet and knuckles to investigate the trespassers. Father and Taneya lowered their eyes and sank to the ground. They were in Sultan's territory now, and he called the shots. Sultan looked them over before sauntering back to a patch of wild celery. He pulled a stalk out of the ground and bit into it.

Father and Taneya exchanged smiles. It was a fine thing to be accepted by Sultan. The big silverback was protector and decision maker for three females, five younger males called blackbacks, and the juveniles.

Taneya lifted her binoculars to search for Winna. She saw dripping leaves, glistening moss, and a sunbird sipping nectar from a flower. Then her gaze rested on a furry black head poking through the foliage.

"I see Winna, Father! She's turned to the side."

Father trained his binoculars on the female gorilla.

The two waited a long time for Winna to shift positions. They were used to the gorillas' slow ways. Finally Winna stood up and moved into plain view.

"Look!" Taneya cried. "She's cuddling a baby! It's adorable! I wish I could hold it."

But she knew that gorillas were very protective. She remembered watching a research student pick up an infant gorilla. Its mother and the silverback charged the student and bit him. When Winna's baby was old enough, it would approach her on its own, just as Nuru sometimes did.

"The baby looks a few days old," Father observed, scribbling on his notepad. "About 5 pounds, I'd guess." He looked at Taneya. "Would you like to name it?"

"Really?" Taneya was delighted. She studied Winna's baby through her binoculars. Bushy black fur outlined its brown eyes and tiny, wrinkled face. "I think I'll name it Raisin because of its wrinkly face."

Father wrote *Raisin* on his notepad. Then he and Taneya spent the afternoon observing the gorillas. Young Nuru romped tirelessly with the blackbacks until he collapsed against his mother to nap. When he awoke, he was ready to play again.

Taneya chuckled. "Nuru is the spunkiest gorilla I've ever seen," she observed.

"Winna has her hands full, that's for sure," Father replied. He stuffed his notepad into his pocket and rose slowly. "We'd better get back to the Land Rover before the fog rolls in." He winked. "Besides, I have a basketball date."

For several days after that, Taneya begged Father to check on group three.

"Raisin's growing up and I'm missing it!" she whined. But Father was too busy tracking poachers in other parts of the park to visit group three again.

One morning Taneya decided to write Jason a letter about Raisin. She had just picked up her pencil when she heard Father's voice coming from the mobile radio base on the kitchen table. She hurried over to listen to it. If he was trying to reach her mother, Taneya would tell him that she had gone to visit a friend. Instead, she overheard him talking to another ranger.

"Caught a poacher," he was saying. "Told him we'd go easier on him if he tells us where the snares are. Apparently he's not working alone."

Static. The other ranger said something Taneya couldn't make out.

"Mount Visoke . . . group three . . ." Father continued. More static. "I'll get there . . . other snares. Check out your area. Over and—"

"Father! Father!" Taneya yelled into the microphone. "Where on Mount Visoke are the snares?" The radio crackled, and Taneya couldn't hear an answer. "Father! Father! Can you hear me?" Static.

Sighing, Taneya replaced the microphone and paced the room. The snares were in Sultan's territory. But it was a big area. Even if she found the gorillas, they might not be anywhere near a snare. It would be ridiculous for her to go alone into the rain forest to check on them.

But Taneya couldn't concentrate on her letter. She tossed down her pencil and grabbed her backpack. Into it she stuffed a canteen, a knife, and her binoculars. Pulling on her sneakers, Taneya dashed out the door to her bicycle. Jason's basketball was in the basket, but since it wasn't in the way, she left it there and pedaled down the service road leading to Sultan's territory.

"Naoom! Naoom!" Taneya called as she approached the bamboo zone. Trampled stems revealed that the gorillas had been there recently.

Taneya walked carefully through the bamboo, searching for snares. Her heart pounded as she remembered Father's warning to avoid the zone when she was alone. What if she stepped into a snare? She imagined dangling from a rope with a broken leg, then plucked up her courage and continued on her quest to save the gorillas.

Approaching the meadow, Taneya announced her arrival. "Naoom! Naoom!" she howled.

She pushed the foliage out of her face and stepped

into the meadow—right onto the toes of Sultan, who had loped over to investigate. Gasping, Taneya slid to the ground. She watched hairy black feet back away then stop as Sultan sat down. She heard Sultan's heavy breathing and bit her lip. She had never been this close to the powerful leader before.

Finally Sultan stood and swaggered away to eat some moss. Taneya exhaled in relief. Then she smiled. It was a fine thing to be accepted by a silverback!

Scratching her ribs gorilla-style, Taneya looked around. Winna was cuddling Raisin as Nuru frolicked around them. He tagged his baby sister, did a somersault, then scampered away to pounce on one of the blackbacks.

Chuckling, Taneya watched Winna scoot after Nuru with Raisin clinging to her chest. Then Taneya gasped. Only 2 feet away from the romping Nuru was a bamboo snare. Nuru's leg would snap if he stepped into the noose. The gorillas would go berserk.

Taneya inched toward the snare, stopping occasionally to lie on her back and pretend to sun-bathe or to pick an imaginary bug off her skin and eat it. When she finally reached the snare, she pulled her knife from her backpack. The blade glinted in the sun.

Sultan charged over to her, screaming. He slapped the ground in warning.

Taneya dropped the knife into her backpack and froze. The other gorillas gathered around. Taneya sighed in frustration. Her father always cut the snares. Of course, the gorillas weren't nearby when he did. But if Sultan wouldn't allow her to use a knife, how would she destroy the snare?

Taneya sat with her elbow on her knee and her chin in her hand. Juba, one of the juveniles, mimicked her. Taneya laughed. She loved the gorillas. She had to save them!

The gorillas broke off tender bamboo shoots near the snare and chewed on them. Nuru jumped up and down, beating his chest playfully. Not to be outdone, Juba joined in. Nuru and Juba tumbled dangerously close to the concealed noose, and Winna nursed Raisin just inches away from the trigger.

The gorillas were clueless. Taneya couldn't wait any longer; she had to do something! She decided to crawl a few yards away and throw her backpack at the snare. She hoped Sultan would blame the backpack—not her—when the noose went flinging into the air.

Taneya crept away, dragging her backpack behind

her. She had just reached the edge of the meadow when her backpack was pulled from her grasp. She saw Nuru bounding away with it, chuckling delightedly. He stopped on the other side of the meadow and tossed it around like a ball.

"A ball!" Taneya's brain went into overdrive. Nuru was going to help her save the gorillas!

Taneya disappeared into the rain forest, crawled a short distance, then stood and ran. When she reached her bicycle, she grabbed Jason's basketball and sprinted back the way she came. She quietly resumed her place at the edge of the meadow, as if she hadn't left. Only now she held an orange ball in her hands.

Nuru scooted over to investigate.

"Look at this," Taneya crooned, turning the ball in her hands. "This is much more fun than a backpack, see?" She rolled the ball a few feet in front of her. Nuru barked in curiosity. The other gorillas gathered around to watch. Sultan kept a wary eye on Taneya.

Taneya reached out and pulled the ball to her. Then she rolled it again. This time Nuru reached out and slapped it. The ball spun. Nuru shoved it. It rolled to Juba, who darted out of its way. Nuru jumped up and down, flashing a toothy grin. He picked up the ball and flung it. The other gorillas scattered, then bounded after Nuru, who was chasing the ball.

"That's it," Taneya encouraged. "Throw the ball farther, Nuru. Far away from the snare."

Nuru picked up the basketball and threw it in Taneya's direction. The ball rolled near the snare. Juba raced Nuru to it. Crawling, Taneya raced them both. She snatched up the ball and shielded the snare with her body. Juba stopped short, and Nuru crashed into him.

"You aren't making this easy," Taneya muttered. She hurled the ball across the meadow.

Nuru and Juba bounded after it. But Sultan had had enough. He slapped them out of the way and picked up the basketball. Taneya held her breath. Grunting, Sultan flung the ball back across the meadow. It rolled into the underbrush yards away from Taneya. She scooted after it on her belly. The gorillas stayed on the opposite side of the meadow.

Here was her chance. She had the ball in hand, and the gorillas were all far from the snare. She took a deep breath.

"And now . . . my best shot." Taneya flung the ball at the snare.

Snap! An empty noose flung into the air. The ball

catapulted sideways.

The gorillas screamed and beat their chests. Taneya dropped to the ground and froze. She heard the gorillas crashing through the underbrush on the opposite side of the meadow. When she looked up, Nuru was disappearing into the foliage with Jason's basketball.

Father returned home late that evening, tired and perplexed. "We caught a poacher who told us where he and his cohorts had set some snares," he reported to Taneya and her mother. "I was worried I wouldn't make it to a snare on Mount Visoke before an animal got caught in it. When I finally located the snare, it had already been sprung. Half a mile away I spotted Nuru up in a tree. He was holding a basketball, of all things."

Taneya couldn't help but giggle. "That was Jason's basketball, Father. I haven't told Mother what happened today because I wanted to tell you both at the same time."

Taneya told her story.

"You could have been hurt," Mother scolded, hugging Taneya.

Father shook his head. "You shouldn't have gone

into the rain forest by yourself, Taneya. Still," he smiled, "I'm proud of you. You remembered everything I've taught you and acted responsibly."

Two weeks later, Taneya bounded out her front door when she heard Father's Land Rover pull up.

"Jason!"

"Hi, squirt," Jason sang, climbing out of the car. "Played any gorillaball lately?" Laughing heartily at his own joke, he handed Taneya a square box.

Taneya eagerly ripped it open and pulled out a new basketball.

"Thanks, Jason! Now we can play basketball together again!"

"You mean you still want to play with me?" Jason asked, his blue eyes twinkling.

"Why wouldn't I?" replied Taneya.

"Oh, I don't know. I thought maybe after playing against Sultan's team, you wouldn't think I was good enough," he teased.

Taneya dribbled her new ball and laughed. "Let's see," she challenged. "If you're nice, maybe I'll teach you a few moves I learned from the gorillas."

Ayasha's Arrow

AN ORIGINAL STORY BY MARY HOULGATE

Ojibway words:
Anishinabe: a group of native Americans who live in central
  North America and speak Ojibway.
Gichigami: Lake Superior, the largest of the Great Lakes.
Gichi-manido: Creator.

On the rocky shore of Gichigami, an Anishinabe girl called Ayasha fitted an arrow to her wooden bow and pulled the bowstring. She turned her back on the tossing waves and squinted into the forest. She locked her eyes onto her target, a slender sapling. Every muscle in her body strained until—*twang*—the arrow leaped from the bowstring and whizzed through the birch and cedar trees. *Thwack!* A hit! Ayasha silently whooped with joy, for nobody must know what she was doing.

"Ayasha! Where are you hiding, little sister? We have work to do!"

Ayasha winced at the shrill voice of Abequa, her older sister. She raced to the sapling, wrenched out her arrow, and quickly hid both bow and arrow in an old, hollow birch stump. Abequa must never know of the hours Ayasha had spent making and shooting her bow and arrow. Ayasha knew what her big sister would say: "An Anishinabe girl with a bow? But it is forbidden! I will tell our father, and he will take it from you!" She could just imagine the scene: her father, tall and frowning, breaking the bow against his knee while Abequa simpered at his side. Abequa was a model Anishinabe daughter, but she would never understand the thrill of shooting a singing arrow to its mark.

"Ayasha, where are you? You promised me a story about Mishosha, the mighty wizard!"

Ayasha's little brother, Binay, tore into the clearing. Abequa labored behind him, her arms full of basswood bark. Baby chortled in his snug cradleboard on Abequa's back.

Binay grabbed Ayasha's hands and pleaded, "Let's

go to Mishosha's mighty cedar tree, and there you can tell me about his magic canoe and his arrow that never misses!"

Ayasha grinned at him. She loved telling stories.

But Abequa snapped, "No stories today. Ayasha must pound this bark." She dropped her load on the ground. "Without bark fibers, I cannot spin twine, and without twine I cannot mend the nets." She gestured to the lakeshore, where a heap of fishing nets lay by their father's birch-bark canoe.

Grudgingly, Ayasha began to pound the bark with a stone, loosening the stringy fibers.

"I will tell Baby stories by myself, then," said Binay. Ayasha watched him carry the cradleboard toward the sparkling water. The autumn wind bent the treetops and made the waves dance.

"Women's work!" she scoffed. "When Binay is older, he will have the glory of the hunt while I sit at home twiddling my fingers."

Abequa smiled smugly. "You are just bitter because you have no talent for women's work," she said, twisting a handful of fibers. "Your fingers are clumsy. You cannot scrape a deerskin or sew a pair of moccasins. And when you try to embroider with porcupine quills—well!—I could do finer work when I was four!"

Ayasha gritted her teeth. Her sister's embroidered capes and moccasins were splendid. Everybody said so. But it pricked like needles to hear her sister's skill praised when Ayasha had to hide her own talent.

As bark fibers flew through Abequa's fingers, her voice went dreamy.

"Those who hunt are glorious indeed. And Ogima is the best of the hunters, is he not? His aim is so steady, his arms so strong!"

Ayasha groaned. Abequa was always mooning over Ogima and his muscles. She called out, "Binay! Come and tell me your stories!"

But the shore was deserted. Ayasha shivered with fear. Where could Binay and Baby be? Abequa just yawned and arched her aching back.

"He has probably gone back to the village for his toy canoe, the little brat. He is as stupid and careless as you, Ayasha." She picked up another handful of fibers and commanded, "Go get the boys. The menfolk have just returned from the hunt and must rest without the chatter of children. Off you go; make yourself useful for once." Abequa bent over her spinning again, smiling to herself and humming a high, whining tune.

Ayasha sprinted through the forest, her cheeks burning. It was not only Abequa who thought she was stupid and useless. Every time she made a mistake in her work, her mother sighed, "What sort of woman will my clumsy, daydreaming daughter become?" But Ayasha's clan knew nothing of her skill with a bow. And so it must remain.

Ayasha slowed as she approached the cluster of birch-bark wigwams. The men squatted by their homes, tired after many days of hunting and trapping. The women were busy skinning game and boiling water. Ogima loitered near Ayasha's mother, polishing his bow. But there was no sign of Binay or Baby.

"Ayasha! What brings you running?" called her mother.

Ayasha wiped the sweat off her forehead. "I'm looking for Binay and Baby," she panted. "They have wandered away from the clearing."

Her father stepped quickly from the wigwam. "If they have wandered too near the water, they may be in danger. I will find them." Ayasha's heart sank. Binay had carried Baby right down to the waves.

"Let me help you!" Ogima volunteered.

"I will look for them in the village," said Ayasha's

mother, wringing her hands. "Or perhaps Abequa has the boys safely with her now." She frowned at Ayasha and waved her away. "Make yourself useful and go and see if the boys are with your sister!"

Ayasha wheeled around and set off running once more. To soothe her stinging heart, she imagined herself an arrow, fleet and sure, slicing through the forest.

When Ayasha reached the clearing, Abequa looked up from the net she was mending. "They were there, yes?"

Ayasha shook her head as she bent to catch her breath.

Abequa knit her brows. "I have called, but they are nowhere in the forest. This is all your fault!"

"My fault?" Ayasha cried. "How?"

"You fill Binay's head with magic canoes and mighty wizards. No wonder he wanders around in a daze!"

Ayasha jumped up. "Mishosha's cedar tree!" she gasped. She sprinted toward the water and along the rocky shore. When she finally reached the tall, wind-bitten cedar at the water's edge, she craned her neck and peered into its branches. A branch fell at her feet. Then she heard Binay's wavering voice.

"Well, I can't see any magic canoes on the lake today." Ayasha heard a scuffling noise followed by a sharp crack. "And Mishosha's tree is not meant for climbing. It's too wobbly for us up here."

Abequa caught up with Ayasha, the newly mended net slung over her shoulder. "Where are the boys?"

Ayasha pointed up to the swaying treetop.

Abequa gasped. "Binay!" she shouted. "Why did you climb up so high? Is Baby with you?"

Binay's voice came shrilly through the cedar fronds. "Yes, we're both up here. Ayasha says that from the top of Mishosha's tree, you can see the mighty wizard paddling his canoe far out on the lake." There was another sharp crack, and the wind twisted the branches wildly. Baby started wailing.

"Get us down *now*, please!" blurted Binay.

"Climb down, little brother! Be quick!" Abequa ordered sharply.

"I can't," called Binay. "The cradleboard strap broke. I can't carry it and climb down at the same time."

Ayasha imagined the little boy clinging to the cradleboard with one arm, his other arm strained around the rough tree trunk, terrified as the wind roared in his ears and the sun on the water glared in his eyes.

Rescuing the boys would be difficult. All the lower branches had snapped off under Binay's feet, so it was impossible to climb the tree. The boys were stranded, twenty paces up. They were too far up to jump down. And all the while, the wind grew stronger, straining the old tree and whipping the branches high over the choppy water.

Abequa grabbed her sister's sleeve. "We must fetch Father."

"There's no time. If Binay loses hold, they'll both fall. Or the branch might break. Or he might drop Baby. We need to get them down now!" Ayasha urged.

Abequa wheeled to face her little sister.

"You and your stories!" She shoved the fishing net at Ayasha. "If you could mend nets as quickly as you weave stories, our work here would have been finished long ago!"

But Ayasha wasn't listening. She was staring up at the tree, her fingers grasping the net's rough weave. She had an idea.

"We must make a rope ladder." She drew out her knife and began sawing the net, cutting off long pieces. "We will throw it up into the tree, Binay will tie it securely, and then we can climb up and fetch the boys."

Abequa, suddenly speechless, nodded. Her strong fingers quickly knotted the pieces together, making the rope longer and longer. The girls worked silently but for the rasp of the knife and the whistling wind. Ayasha gauged the distance and at last said, "Enough."

She tied a stone to the end of the rope. Then she ran to the base of the tree, whirled her arm around, and hurled the stone into the tree. But her arm was not strong enough. The stone went only to the second broken branch; Binay and Baby were still many paces higher. Ayasha tried again. The rope ladder dropped useless at her feet. Panic surged through her.

She must be calm. She must think. And then she realized the perfect way to get the rope high enough: an arrow.

Her mind spun. If Abequa saw Ayasha shooting an arrow, she would tell. Was Ayasha strong enough to face the anger of her father, the breaking of her bow? Could she really make such a sacrifice? But her brothers, clinging to the tree, needed her skill now. If this was to be the last time she would ever shoot an arrow, then so be it. She sprinted to the old birch stump and pulled out her bow and arrow. Then she sprinted back to the cedar tree and tied the rope to the arrow.

"A bow? But how? You mustn't!" Abequa sputtered. Ayasha brushed her aside.

"Binay! Listen carefully! I'm sending up a rope for you. You must tie it fast to the branch above you; make a strong knot like Father showed you!"

"I know how!" he shouted down.

Ayasha fitted the arrow and aimed carefully. She could see nothing of her brothers behind the waving cedar branches. What if her arrow struck them?

"Binay, you must cling to the tree like bark and make yourself small like a turtle. Can you?"

"Of course! That is how I hide from Mother!"

She pulled back the bowstring, straining every muscle, aiming carefully. Her back ached with the tension. Then with a grunt, she let her arrow fly.

Like a swallow the arrow soared higher and higher, the knotted rope flying behind. Ayasha held her breath. Would it reach? Would Binay see it? The arrow disappeared into the tree. Then the rope hung still, its end dangling two paces off the ground.

There was rustling and then a shout: "An arrow! It came on an arrow! I'm tying the rope just right, Ayasha!" The arrow came clattering through the branches and dropped at Ayasha's feet. "Now—try it!"

Ayasha pulled on the rope. It held strong. She glanced at Abequa, who was gaping like a fish. Ayasha laid her bow gently on the ground, near the arrow she was certain she would never shoot again. Then she leaped up and seized the rope in both hands. Hand over hand and foot over foot, she climbed skyward. Prickly twigs tore her skin, and cedar branches poked her eyes. The wind roared in her ears, *Never again! Never again will your arrows fly!*

Finally she reached the boys. Binay, clutching the cradleboard and the tree for dear life, beamed. When he saw her, Baby chuckled. "I tied it right, Ayasha!" Binay said.

She balanced next to the boys and hugged them both, her heart bursting with relief. Then she gathered the cradleboard in one arm and helped Binay climb onto the rope.

"Now we go down again!" she said.

Quickly and carefully, they descended. Binay chattered all the way down, while Ayasha brushed the twigs from Baby's eyes and tried not to think of what Abequa would say.

As they tumbled to the ground, they heard shouts. Several men, including their father and Ogima, were running toward them along the shore.

Abequa gave Ayasha a long, piercing look. She said

nothing, but smoothed her hair and dipped her head to Ogima.

Then Binay shouted out, "Look, everybody! Mishosha's magic arrow must have saved us!" And he held out Ayasha's arrow.

The men murmured. Ogima folded his muscular arms across his chest and said, "It is impossible. For there were only girls here, and girls cannot shoot."

Ayasha's heart blazed.

"The arrow is mine, Father." She lifted her bow from the ground and handed it to him. "I am sorry if this angers you. But I am not sorry I learned to shoot."

Ogima stepped forward. "Hunting is for men!"

Father's face was as dark as a thundercloud. "Ogima is right, Ayasha, as you well know!" And he lifted the bow upon his knee.

"Stop!" Abequa darted forward and snatched the bow. Father wheeled around, furious.

"How dare you! Your impudence will be punished! You both will be punished! Give back the bow at once!"

But Abequa stood firm.

"Please, Father—all of you," she said. "Ayasha was not hunting. Her skill saved our brothers. Could even a man have shot so true?"

They all stared up at the tree. Then Ogima spoke again. "The shot was merely lucky. No girl has the skill to shoot so well."

Ayasha blurted out, "I will show you all! For I have learned as long and practiced as hard as any man!"

She took the bow from Abequa and pointed into the forest. "The birch sapling forty paces to the right of the stump," she called.

Ogima snorted, "Impossible!"

But Father nodded. Ayasha grabbed her arrow, fitted it to the bow, and drew back the bowstring as far as she could. She would show them how a girl could shoot!

With a grunt, she let the arrow fly. It whistled through the forest and bit into the sapling, clean and perfect.

The men stood like stones. Ogima coughed and said, "She must be punished. It is not right for a girl—"

But Father cut him off. "She shoots better than many here. Better than you, Ogima. Such skill is a gift from Gichi-manido; it must be cherished."

Then Abequa stepped up to her sister and stroked the bow. "Please, Father, let her teach me. I would love nothing better."

"You? Shoot a bow?" scoffed Ogima. "But you are a

proper daughter and love women's work!"

Abequa boldly looked him in the eye and said, "I love to do things well and be useful. Ayasha has shown me that a girl who can shoot is indeed useful!"

Ayasha jumped forward. "What if Abequa teaches me to spin and sew better? I could learn from her while she learns from me. Together we could do all our work and still have time for our bows. It is a good bargain."

Ogima sniffed and stalked off. Ayasha and Abequa burst out laughing as he tripped over the loose rocks. The other men shook their heads. "He is too proud, that boy," said one. "We must learn from Gichi-manido," said another. "I am honored to have Ayasha in our clan," said a third.

Father looked thoughtfully at his daughters.

"You two are usually bickering like crows over meat. Perhaps there was magic in that arrow after all! Very well, daughters. You have your bargain."

And so it was, on the rocky shore of Gichigami, that two Anishinabe girls spun twine and mended nets together. When their work was over, they stood side by side and let their arrows fly. And the glorious hunter Ogima? Abequa never mentioned his name again.

Author Biographies

Bonnie Brightman, author of the original story "Firedance," lives with her family in southwest Idaho, where wildfires are a common danger. Her stories and historical articles have been published in *Cricket, Boys' Life, Guideposts for Teens,* and *Chicken Soup for the Soul III* (Health Communications, Inc.). Bonnie's book *Jimi Hendrix* was published by Lerner Publications in 2000.

Marianne J. Dyson based her original story "On the Way to Broken Bow" on the true story of a girl who was burned because she washed her hair with gasoline. With a degree in physics, Marianne was one of the first ten women to work for NASA in Mission Control. She is now a full-time writer, and her first book, *Space Station Science* (Scholastic), won the Golden Kite Award for best nonfiction children's book in 1999. She shares her adventures through her stories, poetry, and appearances at schools and conferences.

Mary Houlgate was born in Ohio and spent her childhood summers on a small island in Lake Huron. She heard many Native American legends then and continued to read about the Anishinabe as she grew older. Mary based her original story "Ayasha's Arrow" on what she's learned. She now lives with her husband and four children in England, where she writes stories and articles for American and English magazines and works as a school secretary.

Tenna Leigh lives in Los Gatos, California. As a freelance writer, she explores many different subjects. Tenna has written for newspapers, magazines, and health publications and is the author of *Understanding and Accommodating Physical Disabilities* (Quorum Books). She is currently working on a picture book and a biography for young readers. Her love of the ocean and lighthouses inspired her original story "Abbie's Light."

Nancy Alpert Mower has written seven books for children and has had stories published in children's magazines, including *Cricket* and *Highlights*. She is a member of The Society of Children's Book Writers and Illustrators and of Children's Literature Hawai'i. Nancy is currently teaching a class in children's literature at the University of Hawai'i. Her original story "The Treasure beneath the Hay," although fictional, is based on a true incident in her grandmother's life.

Timothy Tocher, author of the original story "Reni and the Tiger," lives in New York State's Hudson Valley with his wife, Judy. His stories appear in *Girls to the Rescue Book #6*, *Newfangled Fairy Tales Book #1* and *Book #2* (Meadowbrook Press), and *Cricket* magazine. His humorous poems are published in *Kids Pick the Funniest Poems* and *No More Homework! No More Tests!* (Meadowbrook Press). Timothy's first novel, *Long Shot*, will be published by Meadowbrook Press in 2001.

Debra Tracy, author of the original story "Taneya's Best Shot," is a home-schooling mom who lives in Farmington, Minnesota, with her husband, four children, and Shetland sheepdog. Her stories appear in *Spider* magazine, *Girls to the Rescue Book #5* (Meadowbrook Press), and *Newfangled Fairy Tales Book #2*. When not home-schooling or teaching Sunday school and ESL courses at her church, Debra enjoys in-line skating, playing volleyball, and—most of all—writing.

Penny Warner has had over twenty-five books published for parents and kids that feature ideas for parties, games, activities, and snacks. She teaches child development courses at Diablo Valley College and creative writing workshops at Cal-State University Hayward and the University of California Berkeley Extension. The characters from Penny's original story "Troop 13 to the Rescue" will appear in her novel, *The Mystery of the Haunted Caves*, scheduled to be published by Meadowbrook Press in 2001. Penny lives in Danville, California, with her husband and two grown children.

Look for Meadowbrook Press books where you buy books.
You may also order books by using the form printed below

Order Form

Qty.	Title	Author	Order No.	Unit Cost (U.S. $)	Total
	Bad Case of the Giggles	Lansky, B.	2411	$16.00	
	Free Stuff for Kids	Free Stuff Editors	2190	$5.00	
	Girls to the Rescue, Book #1	Lansky, B.	2215	$3.95	
	Girls to the Rescue, Book #2	Lansky, B.	2216	$3.95	
	Girls to the Rescue, Book #3	Lansky, B.	2219	$3.95	
	Girls to the Rescue, Book #4	Lansky, B.	2221	$3.95	
	Girls to the Rescue, Book #5	Lansky, B.	2222	$3.95	
	Girls to the Rescue, Book #6	Lansky, B.	2223	$3.95	
	Girls to the Rescue, Book #7	Lansky, B.	2224	$3.95	
	If Pigs Could Fly . . .	Lansky, B.	2431	$15.00	
	Kids Pick the Funniest Poems	Lansky, B.	2410	$17.00	
	Kids' Party Games and Activities	Warner, P.	6095	$12.00	
	Miles of Smiles	Lansky, B.	2412	$17.00	
	Newfangled Fairy Tales, Book #1	Lansky, B.	2500	$3.95	
	Newfangled Fairy Tales, Book #2	Lansky, B.	2501	$3.95	
	No More Homework! No More Tests!	Lansky, B.	2414	$8.00	
	Poetry Party	Lansky, B.	2430	$15.00	
	Young Marian's Adventures	Mooser, S.	2218	$4.50	
	What Do You Know about Manners?	MacGregor, C.	3201	$6.99	
				Subtotal	
			Shipping and Handling, see below		
			MN residents add 6.5% sales tax		
				Total	

YES, please send me the books indicated above. Add $2.00 shipping and handling for the first book with a retail price up to $9.99, or $3.00 for the first book with a retail price over $9.99. Add $1.00 shipping and handling for each additional book. All orders must be prepaid. Most orders are shipped within two days by U.S. Mail (7–9 delivery days). Rush shipping is available for an extra charge. Overseas postage will be billed. **Quantity discounts available upon request.**

Send book(s) to:

Name _____

Address _____

City _____ State _____ Zip _____

Telephone (_____) _____

Payment via:

☐ Check or money order payable to Meadowbrook (No cash or COD's please)

☐ Visa (for orders over $10.00 only)   ☐ MasterCard (for orders over $10.00 only)

Account # _____

Signature _____ Exp. Date_____

You can also phone or fax us with a credit card order.

A *FREE* Meadowbrook catalog is available upon request.

Mail to: Meadowbrook Press, 5451 Smetana Drive, Minnetonka, MN 55343
Phone 952-930-1100   Toll-Free 800-338-2232   Fax 952-930-1940
For more information (and fun) visit our website: www.meadowbrookpress.com.

Eight great stories about eight clever and courageous girls!

Once again, girls save the day in these eight exciting, inspiring, and entertaining stories from around the world.

Inside you will find such heroes as:

- Kimberly, a 13-year-old American girl, who must land a plane flying through a storm after the pilot is knocked out and the plane loses electrical power.
- Goldie, a Jewish girl, who helps her family smuggle her two brothers out of Russia to protect them from being drafted into the Russian army.
- Taneya, a Rwandan girl, who uses her wits and her skill at basketball to outwit poachers and to save a young gorilla.
- Reni, living in the Sumatran rain forest, who must dispose of a tiger that has taken away her grandfather's livelihood.

*"**Girls to the Rescue** will please and inspire girls."*
—*Women's Circle*

Bruce Lansky picked the stories in this book with the help of girls ages 7 to 13. He also created the *Newfangled Fairy Tales* series and a series of humorous poetry books, including *Miles of Smiles, Happy Birthday to Me!, No More Homework! No More Tests!, A Bad Case of the Giggles, Kids Pick the Funniest Poems, Poetry Party,* and *If Pigs Could Fly.*

Meadowbrook Press

Intermediate Fiction

Published ... 377-8

GENERAL

60395

9 780881 663778

ISBN 0-88166-377-8

0 76714 02224 9